"No great mind has ever existed without a touch of madness."

The Iron Empire

James Dashner

SCHOLASTIC INC.

For everyone on the Infinity Ring team.
Thank you for making this story come to life.
— J.D.

All rights reserved. Published by
Scholastic Inc., *Publishers since 1920.*
SCHOLASTIC, INFINITY RING, and associated logos
are trademarks and/or registered trademarks of Scholastic Inc.

Library of Congress Control Number: Available

ISBN 978-0-545-48464-0
10 9 8 7 6 5 4 3 2 1   14 15 16 17 18

Cover illustration by Michael Heath
Book design by Keirsten Geise
Back cover photography of characters by Michael Frost © Scholastic Inc.
Detail from *Perseus Killing Medusa* by Wilhelm Janson and Antonio Tempesta, 1606,
courtesy The Los Angeles County Museum of Art, lacma.org
Detail from *Hercules and the Boar of Erymanthus* by Antonio Tempesta and
Nicolo Van Aelst, 1608, courtesy The Los Angeles County Museum of Art, lacma.org
Puzzle rendition of images: Jeremy West for Scholastic

Library edition, February 2014
Printed in China   62

Scholastic US: 557 Broadway · New York, NY 10012
Scholastic Canada: 604 King Street West · Toronto, ON M5V 1E1
Scholastic New Zealand Limited: Private Bag 94407 · Greenmount, Manukau 2141
Scholastic UK Ltd.: Euston House · 24 Eversholt Street · London NW1 1DB

PROLOGUE

ARISTOTLE STUDIED the black and white stones on the checkered *Petteia* board, wondering if it was a bad idea to beat Plato three times in a row. The man might be the greatest philosopher of all time, but he sure got cranky when he lost at games. And a grumpy Plato was never a good thing.

Trying his best to show a look of deep concentration, Aristotle moved a black stone to a square that opened up an opportunity for his teacher to trap him several turns later.

"Going to let me win, are you?" Plato asked, a stern look of disapproval crinkling his ancient face, half-hidden by a ringlet-filled beard. He leaned back in his chair, stroking that grand bushel of hair hanging from his chin. "Perhaps it's time for the teacher to become the student, and the student the teacher, when the student must teach the teacher what the teacher ought teach the student."

Aristotle stared at his master, fighting to keep emotion from his face—fighting the smile that tried to force its way past the whiskers of his own beard. Plato sounded like a philosopher even when he complained about a board game. Several seconds later, after what seemed like a much longer battle of locking eyes, the two men burst into a fit of laughter that would shock anyone else at the stoic Academy of Plato in Athens, Greece. But after twenty years, they had become much more than a pupil and his instructor. They were friends for life.

"I thought I'd at least give you a chance today," Aristotle said. "A win for you might save a pupil or three from being sent to the kitchens to scrub pots."

"Ah," Plato responded, "but it's there that you make your mistake in the line of logic, my dear student. You should have foreseen that I would spot your plan, which stabs my pride even more than a loss, thereby making for an irascible teacher indeed. You can discover more about a person in an hour of play than in a year of conversation."

Aristotle frowned, slightly hurt. "Are you saying that you think less of me, master?"

"Of course not." Plato stood, smoothing out the wrinkles in his tunic. "I'm only reminding you to be wary when you make decisions against an opponent in *Petteia*. Wars have turned on less important matters. Come, let us drink wine and observe the setting of the sun."

"What about . . . ?" Aristotle eyed the board.

"You've tainted the challenge," Plato said. "And learned your lesson. Now, come."

They made their way to a balcony on the west side of the Academy, its view a breathtaking glimpse of Athens and the sea beyond. The sinking sun painted a splash of orange across the thin clouds in the sky, and a salt-tinged breeze washed across Aristotle. He closed his eyes for a moment, enjoying the taste of life, then sat with his teacher, facing the waning day.

"I want to hear your thoughts on the future," Plato said as he took a sip of diluted wine. "We spend so much time in these halls and courtyards speaking of the past, analyzing the present. But lately my mind has been heavy with contemplating that which has yet to come. The world is experiencing an explosion of knowledge and growth, but what path does it follow? Is the destination one to be desired?"

Aristotle took his own long gulp of the sweet wine. This seemed a deep subject, even for his teacher, the *master* of deep subjects — it would be long into the night before this conversation ended.

"Have I stumped you?" Plato prodded.

"No, teacher. I'm only pausing to gather my thoughts before I say something foolish. It is the mark of an educated man to be able to entertain a thought without accepting it."

"Wise words," Plato responded. "Which is why in my company you can speak as you think, because I will never hold you to your musings. We are here to philosophize, and by accident we may change the very future of which we ponder. Or, likewise, we may spew forth nonsense and go to bed frustrated at the effort. As *my* teacher, Socrates, said before, 'I am the wisest man alive, for I know one thing, and that is that I know nothing.'"

Plato grew silent, and Aristotle knew that the man now

expected his student to start spilling his thoughts. Which he did, finally feeling free to share the peculiar musings he'd pondered many times in the quiet of his room.

"I often wonder if the world is part of a fabric, master. Metaphorically, of course. We do, after all, imagine the Fates as great weavers. Perhaps time is woven in a pattern, then, and there are threads of events *placed* in that pattern in some predetermined sequence. And if there is a design to the reality of the universe, does it follow that it's possible for that reality to be . . . broken? For things to go the way they should not?"

Plato had turned in his chair to look at his pupil, a sense of wonder in his eyes. "Please, do go on. You've captured my attention."

Aristotle knew his teacher was sincere, and he continued with excitement.

"As I study the tomes of our history, a recurring thought always comes to my mind — what if something happened that wasn't supposed to happen? Or what if something *didn't* happen that should have? Is it permanent? Is history permanent? Or can we . . . change it?"

"Change history?" Plato asked. "So much said in so few words. I think you've breasted a topic that in truth frightens me, my pupil. Not in a bad way, mind you. But my foundation trembles."

"No great mind has ever existed without a touch of madness," Aristotle said. "And I do believe that the things I've pondered about our past and future walk the edge of that madness. But by the same token, it may be the most important notion I've ever had."

Plato nodded slowly, considering. "What is at the crux of this . . . notion?"

"Progress," Aristotle replied. "Technology. On a scale that is beyond even the furthest reaches of our understanding. What if some day our race advances enough that we could actually manipulate time and—"

A rapid flurry of knocks at the door interrupted his words. Plato, his beard seeming a shade darker somehow, reluctantly ordered whomever it was to step onto the balcony. A young boy—his name was Python of Aenus—popped his head in and apologized.

"I'm sorry, master," Python said. "But there is a message from King Philip, sent by horse. I thought you would want to see it."

Plato sighed. "What would Socrates say at a time like this?"

"Be kind," Aristotle provided, "for everyone you meet is fighting a hard battle."

"Don't put up airs, pupil." But Plato had the scantest glint of mirth in his eyes—a rarity these days. "Bring it, boy, and then get back to your studies. Tomorrow we will begin the Theory of Forms."

Python quickly handed over the small scroll to his master, then scurried back inside from the balcony, shutting the door behind him. Plato unrolled the parchment and read through its contents, his expression never changing. Aristotle knew better than to pry.

Finally, the scholarch of the Academy of Plato—and

its namesake—looked up, eyeing his student. "Looks like our discussion on the madness of the mind and the ability to change history will have to wait until a later time, my friend."

"Oh?" Aristotle hoped it wasn't bad news.

Plato stood, then glanced at the scroll as he spoke. "You've been summoned by Philip to tutor his son Alexander the Third. The future king of Macedonia." Plato looked up once more, a sense of pride behind that beard and those ancient eyes.

Aristotle swallowed, not sure what to think of such a life change. "Alexander the Third? He's still a boy, still teachable. This might be a wonderful thing."

"Yes, indeed." Plato leaned on the railing and watched the dying glow of the sunset. "There are those who say the boy is destined to have . . . *great*ness. It is my sincere hope that you can make sure this is so."

"Yes, teacher," Aristotle replied, excited by the prospect. "I will do my best."

The Horse's Eyes

"THIS IS the only thing I've ever put my foot down about," Dak said, folding his arms and trying his all-around best to look like a dude who meant what he said and said what he meant. "We're already here. No changing your minds."

He faced his best friend — Sera Froste — and his slowly-but-surely-becoming second best friend, Riq Jones. They stood in a dusty, dry alley behind Ford's Theatre in Washington, DC. The year was 1865, the day April 15, just a few hours from what Dak now considered the darkest moment in all of history. Because his hero of heroes was about to be shot in the head.

He had read all about it in a history book he'd pilfered from 1945. Dak knew Abraham Lincoln as a congressman and lawyer who had spoken out against slavery — and been silenced by the SQ as a result. But when the time travelers had fixed a Break in 1850, they had, in a roundabout way, ensured that the great man would go on to do great things. Dak read all about them.

And he couldn't bear the thought of what came next.

"Have you not learned a thing since we started all this?" Riq asked him. The older boy wasn't being a jerk — even Dak had to admit that the concerns over his plan were pretty valid. But this was Abraham Lincoln. *President* Abraham Lincoln. A once-in-a-lifetime chance lay before them.

Sera had been nodding since the first word popped out of Riq's mouth. "He's right, Dak. You mean a lot to me, and I know this means a lot to you. That's why I let you talk me into coming here. But now . . . we just can't do this. We can't. I'm sorry."

"Yes. We can." It took all of Dak's effort to stay still. Resolute. He wanted to save President Lincoln and that was that.

"And risk everything?" Sera countered. "Throw everything off balance? Create a new Great Break?"

Dak boiled inside. "How can stopping the murder of our greatest president be a Break? It'll only help the world get better!"

"It's not about what events are good or bad," Riq said, "and you know it. It's about a pattern, and that pattern being broken. Making reality unstable. The Hystorians didn't say that Lincoln dying was a Break, therefore him *not* dying might very well *be* a Break."

"It could unravel everything," Sera added.

Dak sighed. They'd just saved the Louvre in France from being sabotaged by Marie Antoinette. Surely

Abraham Lincoln was just as important as a dusty old museum?

"So, it's two against one?" he asked timidly, all his bravado gone. He heard horses clomping out on the main street, and it made him picture the president coming along in his own carriage soon.

"Two against one," Sera agreed. "Good thing we're an odd number so we can't get tied up on decisions. Right?"

"Right," Dak repeated. Then he turned and ran, sprinting down a connecting alley toward the sounds of the horses. Forget democracy this time. He'd talk to Lincoln if it was the last thing he ever did.

Sera shouted his name from behind, and the sound of their footsteps followed. Dak knew he couldn't outrun them, so he had to get a little reckless. He burst out into the main street, where throngs of people and horses and carriages and carts were all in motion. Shouts and curses rang out as he bumped and jostled his way across the road, almost getting clomped by a big black horse whose eyes seemed to say, "Hey, idiot, quit messing with history."

Dak swung around the other side of the horse and rider, and scooted his way down the wooden sidewalk, running past shops and tanneries, a post office. He saw a break in the crowd and sprinted back across the street, toward the entrance of Ford's Theatre, where the nasty deed was going to go down in a few hours. He went for the door, hoping it was open, not caring who was behind it. No one played hide-and-seek like Dak "the Ghost" Smyth.

The door opened beautifully.

One minute later, Dak was nestled behind a curtain in the back of the theater, sucking in breaths like a hungry hippo.

∞

After an hour of searching, Sera gave up.

"What a goon," Riq said, leaning back against the wooden siding of a cooper's shop. "It annoys the heck out of me that I've actually started to like that doofus."

"No one says *doofus* anymore," Sera answered absently.

"In 1865? Actually, they haven't *started* saying it yet. Not until around 1960." Riq smiled. "But it's a good word. We should say *doofus* more often. Especially when talking about Dak."

Sera sighed, almost felt tears emerge. *Come on, Dak*, she thought. *Please, please don't mess everything up.*

A beautiful two-horse carriage made its way down the street toward them, and people along the wooden walkways on both sides of the street were pointing and gawking, whispering to one another furiously. Sera knew who was inside even before the horses stopped right in front of the entrance to Ford's Theatre.

Despite everything, she stared in wonder as the man Dak had described so reverently — beard, top hat, lankiness, and all — stepped out of the carriage. Abraham Lincoln had arrived.

2

A Visit with Abe

ONCE DAK had known he was safe from Riq and Sera, he'd slowly and stealthily made his way through the rows of seats, out a door, up a flight of stairs, and onto the balcony where he knew President Lincoln and his wife would be seated. They should be there any minute now.

He heard the voice before he saw the man.

Dak had assumed the greatest leader the world had ever known would have a deep, resounding, booming voice, a voice that could be heard across the entire country every time he so much as said "Excuse me." But that wasn't true. Lincoln actually spoke with a somewhat high-pitched, squeaky sound. Dak decided that just made him all the more likable.

"Our seats are right up here, Mary," the man said. "The good people here at Ford's were so nice to arrange this. A great way to celebrate the Confederacy's surrender, don't you think?"

"Why, yes, my dear. So very nice of them." Dak could hardly contain himself. He wanted nothing more at that moment than to give First Lady Mary Todd Lincoln a big hug.

When the couple reached the little alcove, Dak gathered his courage and stepped out from the shadows. When he did, Mary gave out a little shriek and clutched her husband's arm. As for Mr. Lincoln, he grabbed her almost as hard, making a sound that made Dak picture a poor little mouse smashed by a boot. He couldn't really blame them for the reaction, seeing a geeky kid in strange clothes appearing out of nowhere.

Dak held up his hands, palms out. "Hi there. Don't worry, I'm not here to assassinate you or anything. I'm from the future. Mary, you're looking quite dandy tonight." He let out a little peep of a laugh, and then his face reddened like coals as he realized that he'd just said about the dumbest assembly of words ever uttered by a human being.

The president had regained his composure, however, his face a mask of calm. "Son, is there something I can do for you? My wife and I are here to enjoy the show tonight."

"Yeah, about that . . ." Dak began, searching for how to say this. He'd gone over it, over and over, in his mind while he hid, but now it was all a blank. "Look, I only need a minute. I know this sounds crazy-town, but I really am from the future. And I know something that you *need* to know. There's a man named John Wilkes—"

"Stop." Abraham Lincoln only said the one word, but it held so much power that Dak couldn't have spoken again for a million dollars. Then the man came forward and knelt before Dak—quite the feat, long arms and legs folding up like a wooden laundry rack — putting president and boy on the same level. Then Lincoln reached out and took Dak by the shoulders.

"Listen to me, son," he said. "I can tell you're a good soul, and I'm sure that somewhere you have very proud parents. If you say that you're from the future, then I believe you. But if that's true, then there's a lesson I want you to learn. A lesson about destiny. My path has been laid before me. As has yours. Now it's our job to walk it."

"But . . ." Dak started, but the look on Lincoln's face stopped him cold again.

The president smiled. "What's your name?"

"Dak."

"Dak? Unusual. But I like it." Lincoln stood up, unfolding himself until he seemed to stand a hundred feet tall. Then, looking down at Dak, he said, "Now, go on and walk your path, Dak. Do good things. Make the world a better place."

Dak nodded, suddenly knowing, without a doubt, that Sera and Riq had been right all along. He sighed, feeling that too-close-for-comfort feeling. Not for the first time, Abraham Lincoln himself had saved the day.

"Good-bye, Dak," the president said.

"Bye." It was all he could get through his emotion-choked throat.

Dak walked away from his hero, his heart aching, six words ringing in his head. Six words that he'd never, never forget.

Make the world a better place.

3

The Forest Floor

THE SUN had set by the time Dak came out of the theater, his shoulders slumped, a suspicious redness to his eyes. Sera wanted to scream at him, pound him, lecture him until the moon crossed the sky. But instead she walked right up and threw her arms around him, squeezing tight.

"What happened?"

"You were right," he answered. "Both of you. We need to leave before the president gets shot."

Sera pulled back in surprise. "You didn't tell him?"

"Destiny" was his only response.

Sera glanced over at Riq, who shrugged. At least he didn't say "I told you so," or look smug. The three of them had come a long way, leaving behind their childish ways. Mostly.

"Let's just get out of here," Riq said. "This won't be the best place to hang around in about an hour. And you both know what's waiting for us now."

In answer, Sera reached down to her satchel, where

the figure-eight shape of the Infinity Ring rested, hard and cold. Ready to take them to their final destination, where matters would be settled once and for all.

"The Prime Break," Dak whispered, as if the words were sacred.

The three of them found an alley and walked into the safety of the darkness.

∞

Traveling through the wormholes of time was an experience that Sera would both miss and hope to never do again. She loved it in a way—doing something so scientifically revolutionary, so spectacular, so terrifying. But she also hated it. Every time her body ripped through the dazzling violence of a quantum disturbance, it was as if a part of it got left behind. Time ate away at her like it ate away the years.

Nineteenth-century Washington, DC, exploded away from them, replaced by sound and sparks and streaking light and warping pain. Like always, just when Sera thought she couldn't take one more second of it, they were thrown from the wormhole, spilling out and tumbling across the soft leaves of a forest floor near Corinth, Greece. Sera's head whacked the trunk of a tree right at the end of her roll, a perfect ending.

Dak must've seen it because he was at her side in a flash.

"You okay?" he asked.

She looked up at him. "Yeah, fine. Thanks for asking."

And she really meant it. Maybe Dak meeting Abraham Lincoln had been worth the extra trip after all. Suddenly he seemed . . . nicer. Wiser.

Riq was sitting nearby, arms draped across his knees. "When you get back to the future and everything is hunky-dory and the Cataclysm is nothing but a nice Remnant, I have a feeling you two are going to get married."

Dak and Sera looked at each other, eyes widening by the nanosecond, then they both exploded in a fit of laughter.

"Not quite the reaction I expected," the older boy said.

Sera got control of herself, but lost it when she made the mistake of meeting eyes with Dak again. After another round of the snickers, they finally stopped.

Riq shook his head. "The amount of laughing just now was nowhere near proportional to the humor level. You guys are weird."

Dak stood up, then helped Sera do the same, just like a gentleman and his lady.

"Riq, you've got a lot to learn about life," Dak said.

"Yep," Sera added.

His baffled look made him more likable somehow. He stood to join them just as Sera slipped the Infinity Ring back into her satchel.

"So, what's our mission?" Dak asked, bringing their duties back to the forefront. Suddenly, Sera couldn't bring herself to smile and found it hard to believe she'd been hooting like a tickled six-year-old seconds earlier.

"The Prime Break," Riq answered. "Plain and simple as that. We need to stop Alexander the Third from being assassinated. Sorry we couldn't do the same for Abraham Lincoln."

Dak looked at him sharply, as if he assumed the boy was mocking him, but the expression quickly softened. Riq had been genuine in respecting Dak's all-out hero worship.

"It's a weird mission, you know?" Sera said.

"What do you mean?" Dak asked.

"It's 336 BC. We're in Greece. And we have a mission. But things are so different now. There *are* no Hystorians here. Or SQ for that matter. No Time Wardens. Aristotle doesn't even know about the society that *he* created yet. Or, I guess, creates. It's just strange to think about."

Dak's eyes lit up like something had just clicked in his brain. "If we end up fixing all the Breaks, then Aristotle doesn't even *need* to create the Hystorians, right? So how will our future selves know to come back and . . ."

He trailed off, and Sera knew why. "Pointless to talk about," she said. "It's the old go-back-and-kill-your-own-grandma argument. Somehow, it just doesn't work that way. Time lines, the river, boulders in the stream, all that. Let's just focus on getting the job done. And trusting the Hystorians."

"First things first," Riq said. "Dak, you're the history dork." He said the words the same way he'd compliment a nicely cooked steak. "Give us the scoop on what *did* happen to Alexander, and then we can figure out how to change things."

Dak looked like a kid who'd just been given an eternal hall pass at school. "Well, Riq, I'm a little rusty on the subject, but—"

"Oh, please," Sera inserted. "You know every little fact and figure. Spill it."

"Your wish is my command, my lady." Dak straightened and looked off somewhere in the distance, as if he were recalling an actual memory. "A man named Attalas was behind the murder of King Philip and Alexander. Attalas wanted his grandson, Karanos, to be the next king of Macedonia, and Alexander stood right smack in the way of that. The man who actually did the deed was named Pausanius, a nobleman who'd become a close bodyguard of King Philip. Pausanius poisoned both Philip and Alexander while they were in camp with the army, preparing to march against Asia Minor. Philip wanted to conquer the whole Persian Empire eventually."

Sera felt her eyes starting to cross as her friend spoke. All she heard was a bunch of names and the drone of Dak's teaching voice. Even after all she'd experienced, history just wasn't her thing.

"It should be pretty simple," Dak continued. "If I remember correctly"—Sera almost groaned at that; of *course* he remembered correctly—"Alexander had made a surprise visit to see his dad that day—Alex was actually living with his mom somewhere else. She'd kinda been exiled, but that's a whole 'nother story. Anyway, all we have to do is make sure our boy Alex doesn't make that trip. Then he won't be killed. This might be our easiest Break yet!"

"Don't say that, you goofball," Riq said. "You'll jinx us."

Sera sighed, knowing without a doubt that the odds of things being easy were on par with the odds of Dak going on a no-cheese diet. "So when and where does the murder happen?"

"Three weeks from now," Dak answered, "way up near the northern border of Greece. Just a few hundred miles, NBD."

"NBD?" Riq repeated.

"No big deal."

"Wait a minute," Sera said. "Why are we *that* early, and so far away? Why did the Hystorians have us come to Corinth?"

Dak's face split into an all-too-familiar grin. "I think I know exactly why. Because there's no way we can do this before talking to The Man himself." He paused for a dramatic effect that certainly wasn't needed. "Let's go find Aristotle."

A Doozy

"You know," Sera said, "I've spent most of my life thinking I'd never hear the phrase 'Let's go find Aristotle.'"

Dak was beaming on the inside, and probably on the outside, too. Ever since he'd first learned that Aristotle had been the one to start the Hystorians, he'd been waiting to say those exact words.

"Well, it's our lucky day, isn't it?" he said, then he pulled the SQuare from his pants—he loved keeping it there for the sole reason that Sera made a disgusted face every time she had to touch it. "Now, let's just check in with what our good friend Arin left us on here, if anything. Maybe she knew an exact time and place to find the dude."

"'The dude'?" Sera asked. "That's what we're calling one of the greatest philosophers of all time, now? The dude?"

Dak was fiddling with the SQuare and barely heard her. After he had logged in, a block of text popped up, with a complicated Art of Memory pictogram right below it. *Of course,* Dak thought. Of all the people they'd dealt with, Aristotle would be the one most likely to pass down a cryptic clue concerning the very Break that started it all. He was the source of the mnemonic learning system in the first place.

Dak showed the screen to his friends.

"Oh, boy," Riq said. "That one looks like a doozy."

"Exactly," Dak responded. "Which is why I'm going to take the first crack at it."

Sera reached out and ripped the SQuare from Dak's hands. "Silly boys. How about we all do this together?" She sat down on the forest floor and held the device out on her lap for all to see.

Dak crouched over her shoulder and peered down at the glowing screen. "Should I read the poem out loud?"

"Go for it."

```
A tale I'll tell to all the world,
A tale not true to them unfurl.
To hide the truth, to lead astray,
Those who want the Breaks to stay.
The murders both are vicious, cruel,
An end unworthy, for wise nor fool.
The one who hides behind the deed,
Is one of evil, spiteful creed.
Search the clue to you I give.
Sift it, as sand through a sieve.
Find the traitor, find the one,
Who'd have our pattern ripped, undone.
```

After Dak read it, he scanned through the words again, hoping that something would pop out at him. But it really just seemed like a prelude to the pictogram below it. That's what they needed to solve

"'A tale not true'? So it wasn't . . . what was his name?" Sera asked, looking over her shoulder at Dak.

"Attalas," Dak answered. "Looks like someone *else* was behind the murders."

Riq was kneeling next to Sera, intently studying the screen. "Maybe it'll be obvious once we figure out the clue he left."

"Looks hard," Dak said, half to himself.

Riq nodded. "Like I said. A doozy."

After several minutes of studying the pictogram, Sera finally clicked off the power to the SQuare. "My eyeballs are starting to hurt. Let's take a break and let it simmer in our heads."

"I recognize the images," Dak said. "That's Herakles and Perseus. But they're mythological figures, not historical people. They obviously didn't kill anybody. So what does it mean?"

"I just thought of something," Riq said. "Aristotle *wrote* this clue, right? And Dak thinks the first thing we need to do is meet the old man. So why even bother with trying to solve this. Let's just go ask the source!"

Dak's first instinct was to take an opportunity to point out just how dumb Riq was. But he didn't have the heart for it. After all, for a split second, Dak had actually thought the same thing.

"He won't know any more than we do," he said. "He won't know anything about the murders or who was behind them until it's already happened. That's the whole point of why we're here."

Riq shrugged. "Yeah, but still . . . Once we explain who we are, why we're here, and all that, we can show him what he created. Call me crazy, but I bet he'd be better at figuring out his own clue than we would be."

"But," Dak countered, holding up a finger, "imagine how impressed he'd be if we solved it first."

"I think showing up with a time-travel device will be plenty impressive," Riq replied. "But feel free to tell us the answer anytime you want. Maybe the Greek gods will help you out if you start praying to them."

Sera had gotten to her feet, wiping leaves and dirt from her pants. She handed the SQuare to Dak, who slipped it back in his secret pocket. He knew he must look dazed now, because the wheels had really started spinning in his mind.

"Dak?" Sera asked. "You okay, there, buddy? You look like you're gonna puke."

"No," he replied absently. "I mean, yes. I'm okay." He shook his head back and forth as if doing so would put all the pieces into place. Something Riq had said had triggered a disturbing line of thought.

"Dak?" Sera asked again. "What's going on? Seriously?"

He looked at her, then at Riq, then back to her again.

"I know who did it," he said. "I know who the clue reveals — who was behind the murders."

"That was fast," Riq said.

Sera just raised her eyebrows, waiting for the answer.

Dak felt sick even saying it. "His mom did it. Alexander the Third's mom arranged to have them killed."

5

Son of a God

SERA STARED at her best friend, having a hard time believing what he'd just said. A soft breeze had picked up in the forest, bringing with it the smells of olives and pine. The day had gotten brighter, too, starting to get a little warm.

"What . . . where . . . how did you come up with that?" she asked Dak. "Plus, what kind of mother arranges for her son to be killed?"

The look on his face reminded her of a dam about to burst, trying to hold back too much. "Not many people know about Alexander's mom. Her name was Olympias, and after a few good years with King Philip, they . . . went their separate ways. Which is a nice way of saying that he fell in love with Cleopatra and gave Olympias the boot. He exiled her. She and the kid were sent off to the countryside."

"Whoa, whoa, whoa," Riq said, rubbing his temples. "I might not be the historical genius you are—something you like to remind us about fifty times a day—but I know very well that Philip didn't marry the most famous woman in Egyptian history."

Dak sighed. "Not *that* Cleopatra. She won't be born for another few centuries. This is a Greek woman. Cleopatra Eurydice."

Riq nodded. "Oh. Yeah. Well, see? Maybe I'm good at history after all!"

"Congrats," Dak muttered, then turned his attention back to Sera as if she were the only one intelligent enough to continue the conversation. "Anyway, so her name is Olympias. What does that name make you think of?"

"Greek gods and such," Sera answered.

"Exactly. And she only had one son. And he's the son of a king. Slightly important to her. So guess what she always called him? Her . . . nickname for him, I guess."

Sera pictured the Art of Memory clue left by Aristotle, and then it clicked. She knew what Herakles and Perseus had in common—a father.

"You can't be serious."

Dak smiled. "Oh, I can be serious. She called the kid Son of Zeus."

"Wait," Riq put in. "You mean she called him Zeus?"

"No, she called him *Son* of Zeus. As in 'Hey, Son of Zeus, time to get your jammies on!' Or 'Hey, Son of Zeus, it's your turn to do the dishes!' 'Hey, Son of Zeus, could ya pipe down up there, I'm trying to take a nap!' Son of Zeus."

Riq shook his head. "Talk about spoiling your kid.

I bet he had a ton of friends at the schoolyard when his mom came by to pick up the Son of Zeus every day."

Sera had been leaning against a tree, but she straightened and held her hands up in a gesture that said she wasn't quite connecting the dots. "The fact she treated him like some mythological hero only makes it more strange that she'd arrange to have him *murdered*. Right? Are we sure about this?"

"I don't know," Riq said. "Maybe it has something to do with all that Greek mythology. Those gods were all family, and they were constantly trying to kill one another."

"We just need to find Aristotle," Dak said, pointing off in a direction as if he knew exactly where they should go. "He'll be at the League of Corinth, so I'm sure we'll be able to find him with a little snooping around. I got a plaster bust of him for my kindergarten graduation, so I should be able to recognize his face when I see him."

Sera tried to hold in the laugh, but it came out anyway, sounding like a burp mixed with a cough.

"What?" Dak said, his expression showing genuine offense. "It looked great next to the statue of Michelangelo's *David* that I got for my preschool graduation. Duh."

And with that, Sera started walking in the direction her friend had indicated a few seconds earlier. She didn't care where it led.

∞

Dak breathed in the salty air, enjoying the warm breeze as they exited the forest and walked out onto a bluff that overlooked the city of Corinth. He felt a little burst of pride at seeing the grand buildings of classic Greek design, knowing that it was in this very place that one of the best examples of early democratic government had existed. The famous League of Corinth boasted representatives from every city-state in the Macedonian Empire except Sparta, which had its own agenda.

Aristotle had been a key figure in organizing the League, which for many years ceased the infighting of the Greek states and helped lay the foundation for a force strong enough to counter the Persian Empire. That was, until their two best hopes at leading were murdered by a man named Pausanius.

"Uh, Dak?" Riq said, nudging his shoulder. "Looks like you checked out there for a sec, buddy."

Dak realized he was staring, almost cross-eyed, at the fresco of famous Greek gods adorning one of the larger buildings. At Zeus himself. Son of Zeus . . . Could Olympias really have been behind the murders? It seemed crazy. He could barely keep straight all the things swirling in his head.

"Earth to Dak; come *innnnnn*, Dak," Sera said, stepping right in front of him.

He snapped to his senses. "Sorry. It's just amazing, sometimes, you know. Looking down on actual history." This brought a pang of sadness. "And I still can't bear the thought that everything is changing, getting all jumbled up by what we're doing. I tell myself I'll have the rest of my life to study it, kinda like reading a brand-new book with the same characters. I'll just . . . miss the old book. Make sense? Or do I sound like one of Riq's doofuseseses?"

"No comment," Sera said with a very knowing grin. "It makes perfect sense. It does, trust me. We all feel different weird stuff when it comes to this Hystorian business, but that binds us. We're all weirdos together."

"And that's the sweetest thing anyone has ever said," Riq added. "Come on: group hug."

Dak knew it was weird. Awkward. Maybe the dumbest thing they'd done yet. But he, Sera, and Riq embraced one another in a tangle of arms and shoulders, and squeezed, crushing the breath out of their lungs. A group hug for the ages, right on top of the city of Corinth, Greece.

And it felt good.

The Hegemon

THE HUG had helped Sera feel better.

As they picked their way down the sandy bluff, using weeds as handholds, she kept thinking how close they were. They didn't have to do something so grand and amazing as prevent a mutiny or stop an entire war. This mission might be as easy as warning King Philip or Alexander the Third, making sure they were on their guard. All they had to do was prevent an assassination.

Her instinct tried to tell her it couldn't possibly be that easy, but she held on to hope.

They reached the bottom of the slope and quickly made their way to the outskirts of the town, where some dwellings had laundry out to dry. It was a trick they'd become very accustomed to: good old-fashioned thievery.

"We should really be thankful the electric dryer wasn't invented until 1938," Dak whispered as he pulled on something that looked like a cross between a robe and a toga. He chuckled, that sound that always served as a warning to those who knew him well. "His name was

J. Ross Moore, bless him. He hailed from North Dakota and had obviously gotten sick of hanging his undies on a wire. His prototype—"

"Dak." Sera eyed him, then gestured at the dwellings, reminding her friend that they were standing on other people's property, *stealing* their property, and could be spotted at any second. "Not the best time."

He nodded, not bothering to hide his disappointment. "Remind me to tell you later, then."

"Oh, we will," Riq replied. "No doubt. Soon as possible."

"You see any sandals anywhere?" Dak asked, obviously choosing to ignore the older boy's sarcasm. "Sneakers will not go over well in 336 BC."

"Let's just wear what we've got until we find something better," Sera offered. "These . . . clothes"—she gestured down at the loose-flowing material of the robe she'd pulled over her head—"should mostly hide them anyway. Man, the way these things drag on the ground, I'd hate to do laundry in this place. Dryer or no dryer."

Riq huffed. "Let's just get out of here before some crazy Greek-warrior-ninja comes out and chops our heads off with a scimitar."

Dak shook his head. "I'll pretend like I didn't hear that. It was maybe the most historically inaccurate sentence in . . . history. Come on, follow me."

"You know where to go?" Sera asked.

"I spotted the statue of the hegemon from the top of the bluff," Dak answered, already on the move away from the humble dwellings. "That's as good a place to start as any."

∞

"What the heck is a hegemon anyway?" Sera asked when they reached the main street of Corinth, a bustle of markets and shops and people everywhere. It reminded Riq a bit of Baghdad except that the architecture was so different—all stone columns and frescoes. "Is it some kind of mythical beast? Lots of arms?"

Dak stopped and turned to look at her. "Lots of . . . what are you talking about? *Hegemon* is another word for king. Right now it's Philip. He's the hegemon of the League of Corinth. All the city-states of Greece and Macedonia send representatives here to work through their issues. You know, all that political stuff. It's basically a republic, and it keeps them all from fighting one another all the time."

"Most republics don't have a king," Riq countered. "Or a hegemon."

Dak shrugged. "Well, it was a good start after years of civil war. I won't bore you with any more details." He paused. "Unless you want me to."

Riq had to restrain the look of horror that wanted to pop on his face. "Uh, I think you know the answer to that one. Maybe later."

"Yeah. If you're lucky. Some seriously fascinating stuff."

"I bet." Riq smiled when Dak turned around and started maneuvering his way through the crowds of

Corinth. The kid was a weirdo, but had really become likable. Almost to Riq's chagrin. It had been kind of fun when all they did was fight. He looked at Sera, who knowingly winked at him.

They turned off of the busier part of the street and entered a square with fountains and pigeons everywhere. Things were a little more relaxed here — people strolling about, lovers whispering into each other's ears, friends eating lunch on stone benches. At the far end of the square, a huge statue of a man on a warhorse towered over the people. The man had a laurel crown on his head and a spear in his fist. Beyond the statue was a majestic building with fluted pillars — it was the tallest structure that Riq had seen so far.

"The hegemon," Dak whispered reverently. "And the League of Corinth. This is amazing. If you would've told me when I was seven years old that I'd be standing here someday . . ."

Riq just shook his head. Sera rolled her eyes.

"Some reason you three are here?"

Riq spun around, startled at hearing plain English in such a place. A person stood there — he couldn't tell if it was a man or a woman because he or she was swathed in a loose robe with a deep hood pulled so far forward it obscured the face. And the voice had been muffled.

"Wait," Dak said, tapping Riq on the arm, "was that the translator kicking in?"

"No," Riq answered, alarm bells ringing inside his mind. "That was perfect English, something that no one from here . . . from this time . . . would speak."

"Who are you?" Sera asked, attempting, rather poorly, to throw some threat in her voice.

The person didn't answer, just stared at them through the darkness within the folds of his or her hood.

"Who *are* you?" Sera repeated. This time she did a pretty good job of sounding tough.

Still, the person said nothing. Then, after a few seconds, the stranger lifted the hood and pulled it back, revealing a man with a bald head. Riq took in a quick breath—scars covered the man's face, and one of his eyes was deeply bloodshot, as if every vessel had burst and never healed. The guy was about three doors down from death.

"I'd say I'm a Time Warden," the stranger said, "but you three know that's not true. There's nobody fitting that description at this point in time, now is there?"

"But you could be from the future," Dak said. "If we can do it—"

Sera whacked Dak on the arm, right before Riq did the same. The last thing they needed to do was reveal information to the menacing weirdo.

"Ow," Dak responded sarcastically.

"For the last time," Sera said, "who are you? And what do you want with us?"

"Who I am is none of your concern," the man growled, as if he were an actor in a bad local theater. He pulled out a long, sharp, gleaming knife. "'Cause you're all about to be dead, and I'd just as soon my name not spill from your lips when you meet the devil."

One Punch

INSTEAD OF a rush of fear, Dak only felt impatience. He'd gotten used to bad guys threatening them, and right that second the only thing in the world he wanted to do was find Aristotle. This bald buffoon standing in front of him threatened to delay that meeting, and Dak wasn't going to let that happen.

"Sir," he said, "I know you're holding a knife and all, and we look pretty helpless — at least my companions do anyway — but I'm just going to give you one word of warning. We've been through a lot of junk, and we're the last people on earth you want to mess with. So stand aside or pay the consequences. Your choice."

Sera gave him a look, and Dak wasn't quite sure what it meant. Something between amazement and embarrassment. He figured both applied at the moment. A crowd had gathered around them, and the bald man of scars lowered himself into a crouch, the tip of his blade pointed directly at Dak.

"Tough words for a little man," the stranger said, once

again in that growl that sounded about as authentic as Riq trying to explain the qualities of a particularly gourmet cheese. "Now just watch as I—"

Dak would never find out what the next word to come out of the man's mouth was going to be. Before he could spit it out, Sera had punched the man in the face. Once, hard, a stroke quick as lightning with her fist all balled up like a coiled snake.

The man grunted, then stumbled back, flailing to catch his balance. He regained it a split second before running into the lip of the fountain—then fell backward and made an impressive splash in the churning waters. The people in the crowd around them burst into laughter and applause, just as two men in tunics and armor moved in to take the bald menace away.

Sera held up her hand, wincing with the pain of the punch. "Let's go find that Aristotle guy," she said.

Dak had never been prouder.

∞

Riq couldn't wipe the smile off of his own face, and he hoped he didn't look too goofy as he and his friends quickly made their escape from the fountain encounter with the scary-looking man who seemed to come from nowhere. Sera had shown plenty of grit over the course of their adventures, but punching a man twice her size—that quickly and that fiercely—had taken the cake.

When they felt as if they were far enough away to avoid any further suspicion or questioning, the three of them stopped to regroup. Riq just looked at Sera in awe, but of course Dak let his thoughts spill out a mile a minute.

"That was awesome!" he yelled, dancing back and forth on his feet like a boxer, throwing out fake punches. "I mean, I knew you had it in you, and I wasn't surprised at all, but still . . . So cool! I was about to take care of the poor sap myself, but just as well that you did it!"

Sera gave him an amused look and simply said, "Thanks."

They stood under a tree that was part of a long line bordering the front stairs of what Dak had indicated was the headquarters of the League of Corinth. How someone could know history well enough to figure that out so easily was beyond Riq—but then again, people were baffled beyond measure when they realized he could speak over two dozen languages. Even when he showed off a bit, most listeners still didn't believe—they just assumed he was putting them on with gibberish.

"How much do we need to worry about that dude?" Dak asked. "You don't think he's SQ, do you? Did Tilda get some of her people back to this time somehow? With her Eternity Ring?"

"Seems pretty darn likely to me," Riq responded. "There's no way that guy was a local, and he said the words *Time Warden*."

"Who knows what Tilda is up to?" Sera murmured. Any look of satisfaction she'd gotten from punching the bald guy's lights out had long since faded into grim worry. "We just have to hope we're one step ahead of them. Aristotle was close to Alexander and his dad, so we have an in that she should never be able to get. Let's just find him and make sure we keep this . . . Pausanius from getting anywhere near his target."

"Excellent plan," Dak said. He and Sera both then eyed Riq to see if he approved.

"After you," he said with an ornate, sweeping bow, stepping aside so the other two could lead the way.

Up the stairs they went.

∞

Things were a little different back in the old days.

Sera half-expected the front entrance to have metal detectors and beefy men and women with guns strapped on their belts to watch for strangers up to no good. Not so, of course. Nothing like it — not even an ancient Greek version. Instead they found an open, breezy atrium without a soul in sight save for a man who had to be a hundred years old if he was ten. He sat at a wooden desk, staring at the huge front doors but not seeing anything. He didn't blink or budge a muscle when Sera and the others walked in.

Dak started to approach the guy, but Sera quickly reached out and grabbed his arm. "Are you sure we want to bother him?" she asked. "Better to ask for forgiveness than permission sometimes. Let's just go find Aristotle."

Dak shook his head. "Your lack of Greek political etiquette is embarrassing. Just give me a sec with the old dude, and we'll save ourselves hours of wandering around like dweebs."

"Fine," Sera replied.

"Careful," Riq butt in. "He might keel over dead if you get him too excited."

Dak gave him an appalled look, then jogged over to the patron for the League of Corinth. Sera and Riq followed.

"Excuse me, sir," Dak began. "We're . . . not from around here, but we have some very — and trust me when I say very, I mean very, *very* — important information for Master Aristotle."

"Want to throw in a couple more *very*s?" Riq whispered. "That'll get us in for sure."

Sera elbowed him. She was the only one with official permission to give Dak a hard time.

The old man at the desk acted as if he hadn't heard a word or seen anyone enter the building. His eyes hadn't so much as twitched.

"Sir?" Dak asked. "Can you tell us where to find Aristotle?"

Still nothing. They might as well have been talking to a statue. But Sera could see the geezer's chest moving, although his breaths were very shallow and spaced apart.

Dak shrugged. "Oh, well, at least we tried. So . . . I guess we just start walking around, yelling '*Aristoooootle*, where *arrrrrrrre* you?'"

"That oughta do it," Riq answered.

They moved to go around the man and his desk,

heading for a set of marble stairs behind him, when the old guy suddenly sprang to his feet, fury animating his face. It seemed like an entirely different person had magically replaced the wrinkled zombie who'd been sitting there seconds earlier.

"Stop!" the man yelled, his surprisingly deep voice echoing off the high stone ceiling—in ancient Greek. "None shall enter here who has not sworn the oath! Those not of the League shall suffer the consequences for even attempting such a breach against the hegemon!"

Sera suddenly realized their mistake. The last person they'd spoken to had been speaking English. That meant their translators were only now calibrating to ancient Greek. And *that* meant Dak had effectively been speaking gibberish to the man who stood between them and Arisotle.

A thunder of footsteps sounded from down a hallway to their left. Seconds later, at least a dozen soldiers appeared, spears pointing at the three young newcomers.

"Kill these foreigners," the old man standing at the desk barked. "Kill them swiftly and without mercy."

The soldiers seemed all too eager to obey, charging forward with a chorus of yells.

8

Rumble on the Stairs

DAK FELT like he'd been thrown into the middle of a practical joke. This couldn't be happening. The League of Corinth was about peace, about philosophy, about negotiation, about bettering the fate of man. And now Dak had some old dude calling him names at the top of his lungs and a group of manly soldiers charging at him with big, heavy spears, their points looking sharp enough to gut a half-ton pig.

It all seemed so out of place that he almost forgot to run.

Sera grabbed him by the arm, yanking him back to cold, ugly reality.

They sprinted on the heels of Riq toward the stairs that led deeper into the building. As they rounded the wooden desk, Dak glared at the traitorous old geezer, red-faced and puffing his chest, standing at attention, shouting orders that were drowned out by the screaming soldiers. Dak thought those guys must've not seen any action in a while and wanted to make up for it by slicing three kids to tiny pieces. How had everything gone so terribly wrong?

They hit the stairs and started leaping up them two at a time. Sera had yet to let go of Dak's arm, like a mother shepherding her son. He wanted to rip it free — he was perfectly fine to run from bad guys on his own, thank you. But his smarter side said that he might lose his balance doing such a stupid thing.

Up, up they went, the stairs seeming to multiply the more they ascended. They were only three from the top when something sharp poked Dak in the shoulder just as a hand gripped him by the ankle. He yelped and his arm came loose from Sera's grip after all as he stumbled forward, smacking his head on the blunted edge of the very top step. He had a split moment to be thankful that thousands of feet had smoothed the thing out over the years, then a soldier was on top of him. There was a clatter as the spear the man had held tumbled down the marble stairs. But it was quickly replaced by the nastiest-looking dagger Dak had ever seen — all iron and sharp edges.

A few grumbled words of gibberish came out of the dude's mouth before the translator in Dak's ear kicked back into gear. It had taken a nasty hit.

"—out sliver by sliver."

Dak didn't want to know the first part. He struggled, squirming to get his body out from under the soldier, who had a knee placed directly in the middle of Dak's chest, pressing him into the hard steps below.

"Can't . . . breathe . . ." he sputtered out, hearing the odd echo of the device in his mouth translating the words for the jerk who held him down.

"Don't . . . care . . ." the jerk replied. The dagger pressed against Dak's chin, its pointy tip flicking to draw a droplet of blood—Dak felt it trickle down his neck.

Desperation gave him one last burst of adrenaline. He threw his knee up, slamming into the man and making him groan—a sound Dak knew he'd remember with glee the rest of his life if he somehow survived the mess. Off-balance on the precarious stairs, the soldier fell back when Dak threw all his strength forward in a final shove.

Suddenly free, Dak's elation didn't last more than a half second. Even before he could get a look around him, he remembered just how many of the armed men there had been, and just how big they were. And sure enough, to his dismay, Sera and Riq had been captured by two or three soldiers each, struggling despite having no chance at all. But Dak refused to give up. Kicking his feet until he finally found purchase on the steps, he vaulted himself forward and ran toward two men who had Sera pinned to the ground by her arms and legs.

He yelled—screamed was more like it—as if that would give him any more of a chance. At the last second, he leapt into the air, flying for what felt like a full minute, until he crashed, shoulder first, into the soldier holding Sera's arms. Dak bounced off him like the guy was made of solid stone. He landed hard, feeling as if both his clavicles had broken, trying to focus on the spinning world of marble and stone around him, dread deflating his heart.

Then there were soldiers on *him*, grabbing at his limbs, and Dak reacted on instinct, punching and kicking worthlessly, squirming like a baby who's decided a diaper change is not in the cards. In those few seconds before defeat finally settled in to stay, thoughts flew through Dak's mind:

Had history been changed somehow?

Was the League of Corinth not what he'd read about in all the books?

Had Aristotle gone mad? Evil?

Tilda.

The guy at the fountain, with the scars and the chrome dome.

The SQ.

Had the SQ come here? Messed everything up? Had it all been for nothing?

The spin of questions stopped on a dime when someone punched him in the cheek, sending a swirl of stars around his head, even brighter than the marble on which he lay.

All Dak could do was look up at the soldiers and say the first thing that popped into his head.

"Why are you guys so *mean*?"

9

Behind Bars Again

SERA SAT on a hard floor with her back against a hard wall, looking at iron bars through the scant light of a window she couldn't see. She was alone, her friends taken somewhere else.

It had been a while since she'd had a Remnant. She didn't know why, but assumed it was related to the fact they'd been changing the Breaks one by one. Whatever the reason, she didn't know if it made her feel better or worse. At least phantom memories of parents she'd never met *were* memories. During a Remnant she could see her mom and dad, feel them, *long* for them. And what did she have now? What did you call the memory of a memory?

None of it might matter anyway. She and her friends were once again behind bars—she couldn't help but think back to the tiny, dank cell in the lower decks of Christopher Columbus's ship—and things were not quite what Dak had expected at this so-called League of Corinth. She could tell that much just by looking in her friend's eyes as the three of them were dragged away by those less-than-kind soldiers.

Less than kind. That was *being* kind. They'd all been snakes, bordering on bloodthirsty. How could someone as intelligent as Aristotle have anything to do with such a group of bullies?

Time ticked on. Sera sat, her rear end getting sore, her muscles stiff all over, a bruise rising on her arm from where one of the men had punched her. A young girl. She thought of cataclysms and wormholes and time paradoxes to keep the boredom at bay. Eventually, her eyelids started to droop, and then finally sleep snuck in and took her.

∞

Sometime later—in the middle of a dream where she and Dak were jumping on a trampoline and Dak kept yapping about the "long and sordid" history of metal springs—Sera was awakened by the clank of the door to her cell opening. After she rubbed the blurriness out of her eyes, she saw a soldier standing at the opening, looking slightly abashed. He reminded her of a kid who'd been caught picking his nose.

"Come," he said, looking at the floor instead of her. "Our master wants to see you."

Odd, Sera thought, but she jumped to her feet, not wanting to lose the chance to get out of the rank little prison. When she reached the soldier, he half-turned to leave but then stopped. After a long pause, he said, "I'm . . . sorry."

"You are?" She immediately wished she could take it back, but the words had practically leapt out of her mouth. Why was this big, scary man apologizing?

"Just follow me."

He headed off down a low-ceilinged tunnel, a perfect setting for a dungeon. Sera followed as they made their way through a few twists and turns and up a long, winding set of stairs. Neither one of them spoke as they walked. Sera breathed a satisfied sigh. It felt good to get the blood pumping and stretch her muscles a bit—not to mention seeing brighter walls and light from outside as they ascended from the depths of the building.

Soon, they reached a dark wooden door that led out to a balcony, where several chairs faced the railing and the city of Corinth beyond. To the far left Sera could make out the statue of the hegemon, where they'd met the bald stranger.

Dak and Riq were already sitting in a couple of the chairs, and they turned to see her as she walked onto the balcony. Riq waved, and Dak nodded, but neither said anything.

"Happy to see you guys are safe and sound, too," she muttered. They both smiled as if they had completely missed her sarcasm. She plopped down in the chair between her two friends, wondering if they'd refused to sit by each other on purpose. "So, what in the world is going on?" she asked.

Dak shrugged, his face far too giddy for the situation. He'd obviously been scanning the city, relishing every moment of their latest peek into the past.

"Seems like someone goofed up," Riq said. "A big, burly soldier told me how sorry he was for mistreating us, then brought me here."

"Me, too," Dak added. "My dude was so sweet about it we almost ended up hugging."

Sera stared out at the twinkle of the sea beyond the city, enjoying the breeze that had just picked up. "It's weird" was all she said in reply. That seemed to sum everything up just fine.

Several minutes passed before the person they'd been summoned to see finally arrived. Sera heard movement behind her and turned to see a tall man with salt-and-pepper hair and a beard walk in, his broad shoulders draped in flowing gray robes that made him look like a wizard. He regarded her gravely but didn't say anything as he walked around the chairs to stand before them, his back against the railing.

Ever since the day they'd met the infamous Amancio brothers and Christopher Columbus, the novelty of meeting people from history had slowly but surely waned for Sera. She knew who stood before her, and she waited patiently for either him to announce it or for Dak to blurt it out himself. In the end, it proved to be very anticlimactic.

"My name is Aristotle," the stately man said. "I understand that you had a little mistreatment from our guards today. Let me be the first to apologize. It's not often we get children around these halls, and I think the soldiers got a little . . . overzealous in dealing with such an unexpected threat. If we could do it over again, they might've treated you in a more genteel manner."

Genteel manner? Sera thought. *I guess that's how philosophers talk.* She looked over at Dak, whose earlier expression of glee had melted into a perplexed frown. The poor guy surely hadn't thought his first encounter with the great Aristotle would go like this.

"Why did they treat us like a threat at all?" Riq asked. A bruise on his cheek showed he'd gotten more than his fair share of it. "What did they think we were going to do, bomb the place?"

Dak groaned the very instant that Sera guessed he would.

Aristotle sighed. He obviously couldn't understand the reference to a bomb, but he didn't ask for clarification. "We've had some troubling events of late, and, honestly, I don't feel comfortable speaking about them among strangers. Please don't mistake me. My apologies to you should not be taken as a welcome. I find no reason for you three to be here, and I can't imagine a fitting explanation. But none the less, you are young, and the soldiers should have treated you better."

"We really need to talk," Dak blurted out. "About history and time travel and the SQ and Great Breaks and Remnants and the Infinity Ring and Tilda and—"

"*Dak,*" Sera said sharply, giving him one of the nastiest looks she'd ever had to give. But he'd lost control. "Hardly the best way to start the conversation. He's going to kick us out for being lunatics."

Riq's head was in his hands, slowly shaking back and forth. Their first meeting with the founder of the Hystorians was getting more disastrous by the second.

Aristotle cast a long, lingering gaze on each of the three strangers. His face said nothing, but his eyes were like pools of knowledge, full of wisdom and deep thoughts. Finally, he took a sharp breath and called for the soldiers at the door.

When one of them stepped onto the balcony and asked what was needed, Sera felt a thrilling rush at Aristotle's response.

"Bar the door and let no one through, no matter the cause. I obviously have a lot to talk about with my new friends here."

10

Talking to the Creator

DAK HAD yet to move a muscle from his chair, still transfixed by the fact that *Aristotle* was standing in front of him. *Scolding* him even. He'd always pictured the first Hystorian as a philosophizing dude who sat around reading books and every once in a while pointing his finger toward the sky and saying something wise. But the man who'd just ordered the doors to the balcony sealed was a leader if Dak had ever seen one. A hard, weathered man who'd obviously been around the block a couple of times.

Aristotle moved to the right — the guy even walked with a certain air of grandness — and grabbed a wooden stool, then brought it around so he could sit in front of the three newcomers. After taking a seat, he still towered over Dak and the others, sitting in low chairs. Something told Dak that the man had done that on purpose.

"I wouldn't be here today if I hadn't spent a lifetime trusting my instincts," Aristotle said. "A minute ago, I was ready to throw you out, hoping you'd have been scared enough to never pull such a prank again. Hoping your parents would take you back in and do some serious . . . correcting. But you" — he nodded his grizzled, bearded head toward Dak — "the things you said . . . I can't ignore them. Something is going on here that I want to know about. And I want to know about it immediately. So start talking."

Riq said nothing. Dak looked at him just in time to see his Adam's apple visibly jump up and down.

Sera said nothing. Dak could actually *hear* her gulp.

As for Dak himself, he just wanted to make up for the ridiculous onslaught of nonsense he'd tried sputtering out the first time he spoke. But he couldn't find the words to start.

Aristotle took each of them in with another long glance, then shook his head. "I guess no one ever taught the three of you what the word *immediately* means. Someone speak, or I may call back my soldiers and tell them I was wrong to reprimand them after all."

A burst of courage lit up Dak's heart. "I'll go. I'll . . . try to explain why we're here."

From his right, he heard Sera let out a relieved breath she'd been holding in her chest. Riq reached around her to pat him on the back and whispered, "Go for it."

"Thank you," Aristotle replied. He folded his arms and leaned so far back that Dak thought he might topple off of the stool. But his balance held steady. "I have a feeling you're going to make a bit more sense this time around — you look to be a smart one."

Dak smiled a forced, sad little smile. Had the creator of the Hystorians just complimented or insulted him? Both, it seemed. He took a deep breath and did as Riq had told him to. He went for it.

"Sir, I promise you I've never said something more important in my life—we need your help or the future of the world is in serious trouble. I'm talking, like, lots of people dying and bad guys ruling the world and everybody falling into fiery cracks in the planet's crust as earthquakes destroy the world. That kind of trouble."

Aristotle said nothing, which was the best Dak could hope for so far.

"This is the hard part," he continued. "I know this is going to sound crazy, and you might get up and order those jerks to come chop my head off, but I don't know what else to do but come out and say it and hope that you will be able to accept it." He paused, and Aristotle's bushy gray eyebrows rose so high they almost collided with his hairline.

"We're from the future," Dak finally said, working hard not to let his face squeeze up into a pathetic wince. "Far, far in the future. Like, more than a couple thousand years. As . . . I'm sure . . . someone as smart as you"—he was losing it, he was losing it—"I mean, from what we know, you're the kind of man who wouldn't be surprised to learn that humanity advances far enough for such a thing to happen someday. Time travel. Am I right?"

Aristotle leaned forward, those same eyebrows now crashing down to half-cover his eyes. "Boy, I've said before that the high-minded man must care more for the truth than for what people think. And I can tell you that the number of people in this cluster of buildings who would believe you are, well, less numerous than the nostrils on your face. But if anyone *will* believe, and if anyone will preach it once he does, then you are looking at him now." A huge smile started to form on Dak's face, but Aristotle wiped it away with a quick and sharp look. "*If*, I said. *If*. A word with only two letters, but as important as all the words of language combined."

Dak, in awe of the man's sage words, could only bring forth a nod.

Aristotle turned to Sera. "I think the boy has opened up a floodgate. Let us see if you can channel the waters. Tell me more."

Dak looked at his friend, hoping she didn't mess things up.

Sera cleared her throat, obviously unprepared for the sudden shift in Aristotle's attention. "Um, well, I can vouch for what he said. We used a time-travel device to come here, to meet you, and to warn you about something really bad that's going to happen to—"

Aristotle leapt to his feet and held his hands out to silence Sera. "Now, wait, please. I'm not sure any of us are ready for such a leap. I believe time to be a fragile thing, as well as the fabric of reality from which it's woven, and it worries me to hear of what may be or what may not." He sat back down, his face troubled, looking at the floor as if for answers written in the stone. "My teacher of teachers . . . Years ago, we talked about such things, he and I. I'm not sure if he's known in your . . . time."

"Plato," Dak blurted out before he could pause to think. "You and Plato will be known throughout history as two of the brightest minds . . . ever. You guys are totally famous."

The philosopher relaxed once again, leaning back on his stool. "Like I said, I've always trusted my instinct, and the fact that we still sit here, speaking to one another, means that it has yet to warn me against your words. But . . ." He trailed off, scratching his beard and looking up into the sky.

Dak couldn't let Aristotle make the same choice Lincoln had. If they were going to fix the Prime Break, they needed the man's help. Dak glanced over at Sera, then at Riq. "You haven't said anything yet. Pipe in and help us out a little."

"Yes," Aristotle added, seeming almost hopeful as he focused on Riq. "You appear older than these two. Perhaps we've saved the best for last."

Dak felt a prick of jealousy, and expected a smug look from Riq. When the older boy didn't throw it at him, Dak decided once and for all that their issues were officially a thing of the past. At least for a few minutes.

"Listen," Riq began as he leaned forward and put his elbows on his knees. "This is really hard for all of us, I think. It makes me feel better that you seem so worried about time and messing it up. It shows you get it. But we're here to tell you that things are *already* messed up. With . . ." He faltered for a second, looking to Dak and Sera for support, then surging ahead. "With your permission, we want to tell you about the future. Because we need your help to make things right. You'll just . . . have to trust us that it's okay to talk about. But we won't until you say it's okay."

A long moment of silence passed, Aristotle passing his eyes from Riq to Sera to Dak, then starting all over again. And again. Dak could almost see the wheels spinning behind those eyes.

"I've made my decision," the man finally said. "I want you to tell me everything you came here to say. And then we shall see where we are and what may come."

Sera and Riq both looked at Dak. It was his moment to shine.

11

The Python
Interrupts Again

AND SO Dak went at it, spilling everything in a torrent of information that barely left him time to take proper breaths. About the Great Breaks, Aristotle's belief that they needed to be corrected, his belief in eventual time travel, how the Hystorians came into existence because of his vision, the SQ . . . everything. After he'd told the story of the far future and how he and his friends had been sent back in time to set things right — and to find his missing parents — he quickly went through the list of the Breaks they'd conquered so far. And then it was time for the kicker. The final task.

"In three weeks," Dak said, "an assassin is going to kill King Philip and his son Alexander the Third." The look of complete horror that transformed Aristotle's face made Dak stop before he went any further.

The man appeared as if he might cry. His lip trembled, his eyes grew dark, his entire body seemed to shrink.

"This can't be," he said, his steady, regal voice cracking

for the first time. "I taught the boy, practically raised him through the better part—the most important part—of his youth. He's . . . destined to do great, great things. Change the world. I know it, in my heart, without any doubt. This . . . this can't *be*."

Dak had expected the philosopher to be troubled, but the reaction went far beyond his wildest expectations. Aristotle looked like a man who'd just been told his son had been killed. Which, evidently, was for all intents and purposes what had happened. The man was visibly traumatized.

But then he composed himself, the stately leader and teacher regaining his footing. He stood tall, brushed at his robes, then sat back down again, ramrod straight, looking as if he'd never been bothered at all. Dak's admiration grew.

"Your words ring true," Aristotle said, "and if this truly did . . . or does . . . happen, then my reaction is exactly as your Hystorians have taught you. Such a thing would devastate me, indeed, and I'd do anything to reverse that course." He paused. "We've had trouble lately. Strangers appearing, wreaking havoc. Strangers who are nothing like Greeks or Macedonians at all."

Dak and his friends exchanged looks. The dude at the fountain. Tilda was up to something, no doubt.

"It's why my guards have been so vigilant," Aristotle continued. "So vicious. I ordered them to be so. I wasn't about to let anything get in the way of the League and our plans for this great nation and the world." His eyes found Sera's. "Can you show me the device? Your words *do* ring true, but it would be foolish for me not to have the proof of it."

Sera was digging through her satchel before he'd even finished his last sentence. Dak found he couldn't wait for the philosopher to hold a piece of the future, right there in his hands.

The Ring was dented but shiny, and it glowed with an inner light. Dak knew there could be no doubt such a thing came from a distant future. Aristotle held the device, turning it over and over, studying it with a look of pure wonder.

"Oh, that my master was still here with us," the philosopher said. "If Plato could have seen this, he and I would have spent a year and a day talking over it. I miss the man. I miss him like my own father." He finally — almost reluctantly — gave it back to Sera. "Tell me more of what you know about Alexander's death. If the only thing you've come here to ask of me today is to prevent my student from being murdered . . . Well, you could have saved your breath about all the rest. I would do anything for that boy. Though he's a man now, I suppose. A man grown, and a great one at that."

A rush of excitement had started to fill Dak's bones. They were on the cusp now — the cusp of finishing what they'd started for the Hystorians. It was right here for the taking. With Aristotle's help, stopping the assassin should be relatively easy. If nothing else, the philosopher could just tell his former student to stay hidden in the wings, to avoid seeing his father for a while.

They could do this. They could really do this! Prevent

the Cataclysm. One look at Sera and the light in her eyes showed she was thinking the same thing.

Riq spoke up. "Like Dak said, it's supposed to happen in about three weeks. The assassin, Pausanius, plans to kill King Philip with poison, right there in his big ol' tent where he and his army are camped, preparing for their huge assault on Asia Minor. The oopsie part is that Alexander will be there, on a surprise visit, and Pausanius will end up killing them both."

"Now, wait a moment," Aristotle said, leaning forward with a look of worry on his face. "Two concerns. One, Pausanius seems an unlikely man for the job. He's been a loyal bodyguard for Philip for years. He must be manipulated by someone else. And I would wager every minute I ever spent with Plato that Attalas is the man behind the murder. He's been ambitious from day one for his grandson, Karanos, to become the hegemon some day. And it would do him no good unless he killed both Philip *and* Alexander."

"Which is exactly what happens," Riq rebutted.

"Yes, but you said that Pausanius didn't know — *doesn't* know I should say — that Alexander will be there. If this is about installing Karanos as king, I highly doubt the conspirators would plan the attack unless they knew for sure that both father and son would fall together. I can promise you that they would never have another opportunity after one murder or the other done alone."

Dak was itching — almost literally — to take over from there, but with some spark of kindness dredged up from the bottom of his depths, he let Riq have the fun.

"That's the key, sir," Riq said. "According to our history books, everyone agrees with you and thinks that Attalas is behind the murder, but it's a cover-up. The true mastermind is Olympias."

"The boy's *mother*?" Aristotle asked in a rage, almost as if he'd been accused himself.

Riq nodded, and so did Dak when the philosopher looked at him for confirmation of the shocking news.

"She was even more ambitious than Attalas," Sera added. "She wanted Alexander to be king, and she wanted it immediately. She didn't want to wait for Philip to die or be killed. The plan obviously backfires."

Dak felt like he had to throw something out there. "As for Pausanius, it's true he is the king's bodyguard, but a lot of people will do anything for the right money. Or for power. We've learned that the hard way."

Aristotle scratched his beard. "My heart can scarcely bear it. I love Olympias as well. She is a sweet, sweet woman, who thinks the world of her son."

"Sounds like a Shakespeare play," Dak mused. "Mother arranges for her son to be king, but her schemes end up killing him."

"Shakespeare?" Aristotle repeated.

"Never mind."

Sera rubbed her hands together. "So . . . you probably have a lot of influence with Alexander still. Right? All we need to do is make sure you keep him away from his father and away from Pausanius."

"Yeah," Dak said. "Easy-peasy." He wasn't sure that translated too well because the philosopher's eyes wrinkled up in confusion.

But then the man let out a huge breath and leaned back in his stool once again. "So be it. As I've said, I'll do anything to prevent this murder. I didn't spend all those years teaching Alexander just to have him poisoned by a traitor's hand. I'll have my people contact him first thing in—"

The door to the balcony burst open, slamming against the wall and rebounding to knock a man almost clear off his feet. He had black hair and a studious face, which was now lit with something close to terror. His skin was milky pale. Recovering his composure—only slightly—he more gently pushed the door all the way open, then stared at Aristotle expectantly. The philosopher had stood up, and Dak saw a bit of worry bleeding through the man's normally graceful demeanor.

"Python," Aristotle said. "The last time you so interrupted me upon a balcony, it was for great news. Something tells me the winds blow a different and darker direction today."

The newcomer looked even graver than when he'd first burst in. "Teacher, I'm afraid I have horrible, horrible tidings." He gave a wary look at the three young strangers sitting in the balcony chairs.

"Don't worry about them," Aristotle urged. "Just spit it out, now. What's happened?"

Python's eyes brimmed with tears. "Your former stu-

dent Alexander. Alexander the Third. Son of our great
hegemon—"

"Yes, I know who he is!" the philosopher snapped.
"Is he in danger?"

Python swallowed and his eyes fell to the floor. "He's
been murdered. Killed by a woman with hair of flames
and lips of tar."

∞ 12

Predicament

SERA HAD never felt so stunned by someone's words. She sat in her chair and stared at the man named Python, wondering if she had heard him correctly. More like, *hoping* she hadn't. They were supposed to have three weeks to prevent the Prime Break from happening. And the woman with hair of flames . . .

"You're certain of this?" Aristotle asked his servant, after what felt like a very long silence.

Python nodded, grim-faced. He obviously didn't enjoy being the one to relay such an awful message.

Aristotle slumped back onto his stool, every ounce of blood having drained from his face. Even his beard seemed to sag and wilt, along with the rest of his countenance. "How certain, Python? I must know."

"They have his body, my master. There can be no doubt."

"Then leave us."

Sera expected the man to be thrilled to get out of there, but, impossibly, he looked even sadder. "Yes, teacher. Please let me know if there is anything I can do." Python bowed and left, closing the door as he went.

"He's been so good to me," Aristotle whispered, staring at the stone of the balcony floor. "Been with me for so many years. I should treat him with more kindness."

It seemed like an odd thing to say, but Sera felt a little disoriented herself. She knew they had a billion things to talk about now, but she couldn't find one word to utter. In fact, no one spoke for a good long while.

"What're we going to do?" Riq finally asked, a simple enough question. The answer, not so much.

"Need I ask the obvious?" Aristotle responded. "You came here, told me of an elaborate future wrought with difficulty, and showed me a device that my own eyes are wise enough to tell me is not a ruse. I believe that you three are from another time and place. And yet, you sat there and told me the details of a murder that was to happen three weeks from now. You've thrown my mind into a cloud of doubt and mistrust, I must say." He looked apologetic as he said it, as if he didn't want to disappoint them. But Sera knew he had every right to think them a bunch of liars now. For all he knew, they were in league with Alexander's murderer.

"It's Tilda," Dak said. Sera and Riq had been thinking it—what else *could* they think—but Dak was the first to throw it out there. "We all know it. She came back and took care of business herself before we could even have a chance to fix it. I swear I'm gonna rip every red hair off that woman's head next time I see her."

"That'll teach her," Riq muttered under his breath.

"Tell me of this Tilda," Aristotle said. "Tell me everything."

For once, Dak didn't seem too eager to spew any information from his over-clogged head, but he did so anyway.

"Tilda is also a time traveler," he said. "But she's with the SQ — the bad guys. She wants the Breaks to happen, because each and every one leads to a future where she's rich and powerful, never mind the consequences. Alexander's death is the event that leads to the creation of the SQ. She made sure it happened before any of us would expect it. She beat us at our own game!"

"And what does that mean for us?" Aristotle asked.

Sera answered, unable to prevent her mind from picturing the Remnants of her parents, and thinking how the chance of ever seeing them again — of ever getting to know them — might have just been squandered.

"It means despite our best efforts, the fabric of time and reality has just been . . . ripped, torn. Broken. Tilda has set off a chain reaction that will one day be too much for physics to handle anymore."

"And then comes the Cataclysm," Dak added.

"Yep," Sera agreed sadly. "The end of the world."

Aristotle was studying them intently as they spoke. "But you were able to fix these other Breaks, correct?"

Sera nodded.

"Then maybe having just one go wrong won't be too much. Maybe . . . Oh, what am I saying. Right now my heart doesn't care a bit about all of that. I've lost one of the most precious people I've ever known."

And then, shocking everyone, Aristotle — the great and majestic philosopher, master of ethics, teacher, scientist, poet — broke down and started bawling, chest hitching with sobs, tears streaming down his face into that famous beard.

Sera didn't know what else to do. She got up and pulled the man into a hug. He certainly didn't respond, but he didn't pull away either. The episode lasted for just a minute or two and then he regained his composure. Sera went back to her chair and sat down, looking at Dak, then Riq. They had to decide what to do, but in everything they'd been through so far, no matter how awful, at least they'd had Hystorians and clues and guides as to what to do next.

Not so now. They were at the end of the line, and all bets were off. Like never before, Sera and her friends were totally, completely on their own.

"You know what we have to do, right?" Dak asked.

Sera did, but the very thought terrified her. "You want to go back in time again. Stop Tilda before she can kill Alexander. But it throws all our plans off — how do we know we won't alter history even worse? Or set reality up to break a thousand more times? This is uncharted territory."

"Yeah, it is," Riq agreed. "But what else are we going

to do? Say 'Oh, well' and just go back to the future, hang out on the back porch until our house falls into a river of exploding lava?"

Sera sighed. "Of course not. I'm just saying it's scary and we have no idea what to expect. This isn't a video game we can just reset."

"Why are you being so negative?" Dak shot back. In all the years of their friendship, she thought it might be the first time he'd ever truly hurt her feelings. She felt his words like a dagger. "We all know there's no choice here. Alexander is dead, and Aristotle told us" — he eyed the philosopher with a You-know-what-I-mean glance — "that his dying is the first Break. The Prime Break. The Break that started it all. So nothing else matters. There's no decision to make. We go back and we save him. Boom, that's it."

Sera wanted to strangle him for sounding so arrogant. The only problem was that her best friend was totally right. What else *could* they do?

"Well?" Dak pushed.

"Quit acting like you just found the cure for cancer," Riq muttered. "We all know that's what we have to do."

Sera nodded, refusing to let her pride get in the way. She knew that part of her problem was worrying about her parents and the Remnants. It scared her to death to stray from the plan that had seemed to be leading her to an actual reunion with them in the future. But she was being stupid. If the Hystorians were right, then Alexander's death presented a much bigger problem. It had to be undone, no matter what the cost.

Dak seemed to sense he'd been a little forceful. "What do you think we should do, Sera?"

"Go back. Stop Tilda. You're right." There, she said it. And the way he nodded in response saved her from any more wounded pride.

Riq clapped his hands once, loudly, then stood up. "Then let's get on it."

Aristotle rose as well, very slowly, looking back and forth between the other three with a very uncertain expression. "Are we . . . sure about this?"

Sera and her two friends nodded immediately.

The philosopher straightened and appeared much more confident. "Then I'm going with you. And I don't want to hear any argument about it. I'm going and that's that."

Dak blew a loud breath through his lips. "Why would we argue? We need your help, dude."

The translator didn't like that last word so much — it sounded more like a burp.

Aristotle started walking toward the balcony door. "We'll find out everything we need to know from Python, and then off we go. I just hope that toy of yours actually works."

∞

If Dak could've chosen anyone to go on a time-traveling adventure with, it was a no-brainer that it'd be Abraham Lincoln. But Aristotle was a pretty good second choice.

After talking to Python for an hour or so and learning everything they possibly could about the details of what had happened, Dak, Sera, Riq, and the philosopher were ready to go back in time—they'd decided on three days to be safe—and stop Tilda.

The lady with hair of flames and lips of tar.

It made Dak think of Medusa, who was *almost* as bad as Tilda.

They stood on a patch of dirt behind the official stables of the League of Corinth. The sun had started to set in the west, and Aristotle said that he highly doubted there'd be anyone around.

In the waning light of day, the philosopher stared at the Infinity Ring as Sera pulled it out. "I've programmed in the time and the location," she said.

Olympias's palace, Dak thought. *The home of Alexander and his mom.* Back when this had all begun, if he'd made a list of one million places they might have to visit throughout history, that one probably wouldn't have made the list.

"Is this going to hurt?" the philosopher asked as he put his hand on the cool metal of the Ring.

"No," Sera answered simply. Dak didn't know if that was the most honest answer ever, but it seemed to make their famous friend feel better.

They stood in a circle, the sky above them fading from orange to purple, four right hands clinging to the Infinity Ring in the middle of their group. Sera ignited the device into action and sparkles of light flashed in the air.

Just before they were swept away, something happened that made Dak's stomach almost leap through his throat and out of his mouth. About twenty feet away from where they stood, four people suddenly appeared, almost as if they were falling out of the sky, their images flashing into existence just long enough for Dak to see who they were.

Himself.

Sera.

And a man and woman he'd never seen before.

It was only for an instant, but enough for Dak's mind to explode with confusion. He was staring at *himself*, and the other version of him looked back with an odd expression of understanding. It was unnerving, confusing, and Dak didn't like it one bit.

Then the sky ripped open and sucked them into the oblivion of a wormhole.

13

The Gardens of Olympias

RIQ COULDN'T believe what he'd just seen. It happened so quickly he thought that he had to have imagined it, that he was seeing things in the moment before they were sucked into the wormhole.

He didn't love the feeling of his body being pulled and stretched and compressed by a billion forces all at once, but at least he'd grown somewhat used to it. Not to mention the sounds and the lights and the wind that wasn't really a wind. But he couldn't help but feel sorry for Aristotle—who wasn't exactly young and spry—as they traveled through the space-time continuum.

Like always, Riq had a hard time comprehending just how long it took for them to make the leap. Only moving three days, you'd think it would be a quicker warp than usual. But it didn't always seem to work that way. Regardless, there was the mind-numbing intensity of it all, the world exploding and contracting and streaking all around him, and then it was over.

He tumbled onto a bed of short-cut grass, then

slammed into a big green hedge with prickly leaves. The whole thing shook above him as if it were laughing. Dak's foot smacked him in the face, and he heard Sera asking Aristotle if he was okay. The man coughed, then groaned, then *laughed*. He actually laughed.

Riq got to his feet and brushed himself off, relieved to see the great philosopher doing the same thing, all in one piece and with no obvious injuries. The man looked as excited as a kid at a birthday party, practically floating.

"Oh, if Plato could see me now!" he yelled, obviously forgetting that they were supposed to be on a stealthy mission to save his former student. "Aristotle, traveler of time!" Riq was pretty sure he'd never seen anything quite so ridiculous as the great philosopher dancing on his toes and making such a pronouncement.

Sera was smiling, and Riq instantly knew that she hadn't seen what he'd seen. Dak couldn't have looked any more opposite from her — troubled and confused — which meant that he *had* seen it.

Dak and Sera's duplicates. And two strangers.

And no Riq.

What exactly did that mean?

"I hate to dampen the party atmosphere," Riq said, "but we have to stop Tilda *and* I think Dak and I saw something that you guys didn't." He went on to describe what he'd seen.

Dak's face was pale — seeing himself had obviously shaken him up a bit. "It was weird." Riq had to admit that although the kid didn't have his language expertise, that summed it up perfectly. Sera didn't even bother with the standard doubtful comebacks.

"Who do you think the man and woman were?" she asked.

"Explain what they looked like," Aristotle added, his elation from a moment earlier popped like a balloon.

It had only been an instant, but Riq could still see them in his mind. "The man had brown hair, tall. The lady had black hair, green eyes, thin face, some kind of weird jewel on a necklace around her neck."

"Was it an amethyst?" the philosopher asked.

"*Umm*, no idea." Riq was a translator, not a geologist. "But I think it was purple."

Aristotle shrugged, a comical thing to see on such a great man. "An amethyst, then. The woman you saw was Olympias, Alexander's mother. In fact, we may be meeting her any second now." His eyes focused on something behind Riq's shoulder.

Riq turned around and finally got a good glimpse of the space beyond the giant hedge he'd plowed into upon arrival. Before them lay a vast expanse of gardens — green grass and bushes and flowers and fountains and trees — all arranged in a maze of sorts that reminded him of something out of a fantasy novel. Beyond that there stood a massive house built in the Greek style, with pillars and frescoes and friezes. Small statues lined the walkway that led from the main fountain to the stairs below the back entrance to the palace.

Palace.

That's definitely the right word, Riq thought. Alexander had some sweet digs.

"Philip is a rich man," Aristotle said, looking on with the rest of them at the grand structure. "Let's just say this is his way of keeping his former wife happy."

Dak started to say something, but before he could even get one word out, a door burst open on the side of the palace and three men came charging out with swords in their hands. Three huge, vicious black dogs, barking and growling, followed on their heels, and then one of the guards shouted, his voice a boom of thunder.

"There they are! Appeared out of nowhere! Sic 'em, hounds, sic 'em!"

∞

Dak had always thought dogs were cute. These things weren't dogs. These things were big, hungry monsters that wanted to eat him alive. And with his luck, he would probably be the tastiest of his friends.

"Aristotle!" he yelled. "Tell them who we are!" He'd expected to fight Tilda, but not the people they'd come to save from her.

The philosopher appeared to think for a second about shouting at the men with the swords, but then gave up. Those nasty dogs were charging in way too fast.

"I think at times like this it may be wisest to run," he said. Even on the cusp of death-by-slobbery-fangs, the dude sounded like a philosopher.

"Run!" Dak yelled, getting to the point a lot more

quickly. But then he saw that Riq and Sera had already done that, heading for an area with a bunch of those tall hedges — maybe thinking they could find a place to hide. Aristotle took off after them, lifting his robes like a lady in a dress tiptoeing through a mud puddle. He was fast for an older guy.

Dak took a step to go in the same direction, but then the dogs were on him, seeming like they'd leapt ahead at an impossible speed. The beasts got between Dak and the rest of his friends, and to his chagrin they all decided they wanted to focus on the history nerd.

For some reason the words *sweet meat* ran through his head as he froze, staring at the hideous, slavering monsters, who stared right back at him, their thick throats vibrating with deep growls.

"Nice pups," Dak said, slowly backing away. They inched forward, matching his movement, telling him with their eyes that he'd better stay put if he wanted to live another five minutes. Out of the corner of his eye, he could see that the guards themselves were sprinting through the gardens, almost on him.

Dak held his hands up to the sky, as if someone had a gun pointed at him. "I'm a good guy!" he yelled. "I'm here to save —"

The dogs didn't like him talking. All three of them jumped forward, jaws snapping.

A horrible shriek escaped Dak's throat as adrenaline exploded inside of him. He dove to his left and rolled, barely avoiding the teeth of the lead dog. Then he was on his feet, scrambling around the corner of the original hedge they'd all rolled into when the Infinity Ring warped them there.

The howls and barks of the dogs sounded behind him, and he swore he could feel their breaths on the back of his neck. Dak ran as hard as he could, knowing that he had zero chance of outrunning the drooling monsters. He rounded another corner and saw a big stone dais that had a statue of Plato standing on top of it. It was his only chance.

He jumped onto a small square ledge at the bottom, then vaulted himself onto the dais itself. One of the dogs got the bottom of his robe in its mouth, but Dak was able to rip it free, then climb a little higher onto Plato, who didn't seem to mind too much.

Dak was just high enough to stay alive. Below him, the dogs leapt and barked and snapped those sharp teeth at him.

"Nice pups," Dak repeated, feeling about as ridiculous as he ever had before in his life. He wondered for a moment whether these beasts might be the ancestors of his old friend Vígi.

Just then one of the soldiers arrived — the others must have pursued Aristotle and his friends. The man was young, only nineteen or twenty by the look of it. Dark, curly hair covered his head, and eyes of steel — one blue and one brown — looked on Dak with anger. The guy had a breastplate that gleamed, and huge muscles in all the right places. One tough dude.

"I swear I'm a good guy," Dak pleaded, his arms getting tired from clinging to the statue.

"I bet you are," the guard responded. He hefted his bright, shiny, sharp sword and pointed it at Dak. "But I'll never become Alexander the Great if I believe the lies of my enemies."

Dak's jaw dropped even as the man he was supposed to save stepped forward to kill him.

14

A Golden Throne

SERA WALKED briskly beside Aristotle, Riq, and two of the three guards who'd come bursting out of the house with the dogs. It hadn't taken long for the philosopher to convince them that they meant no harm. But they still had a problem. There was no sign of Dak, and no sign of the dogs, who'd looked awfully hungry when they'd chased him through the gardens.

"I hope Dak isn't dog food," Riq muttered as they searched the hedges for their friend.

Sera smacked him on the arm. "Not funny."

"It's kinda funny," he responded. When she gave him a look of death, he laughed. "Don't worry. Do you really think they'd just let their dogs kill a young boy playing in the yard? I'm sure he's —"

He stopped when they turned a corner of towering hedges and saw the scene before them. If Riq had thought things were funny before, now they might seem hilarious, though Sera just felt a swelling of relief.

Dak hung on a statue of a man, his hands gripping the

arms and his legs wrapped around the torso. The dogs were at the base of the dais on which the statue stood, barking and chomping, slobber flinging in all directions. And then there was a soldier, tall and strong, holding a sword so that its tip rested right under Dak's chin. But the guard was grinning, and it was obvious he had no intention of actually cutting the boy's throat. The young man was probably just trying to teach a lesson, and maybe enjoying it a little too much.

"Alex," Aristotle said in a commanding voice. "Put down that sword this instant! And call off these bloodthirsty dogs before someone gets a foot bitten off."

Riq snickered beside Sera, and instead of smacking him this time she joined in, hoping Dak didn't notice her laughing.

One of the other guards went up and barked some orders at the dogs — he actually sounded a lot like them — and they suddenly ran off, not seeming so violent anymore. Alex — and Sera could only assume that this was the person they'd come over two thousand years into the past to save — stepped back and lowered his sword, a huge smile spreading across his handsome face. Dark curls bounced as he swung his head to see his former tutor.

"Master," he said. "You should really send word before you come to visit Mother and me." His initial glee was dampened a bit by a dark look. "I also trust you'll have an explanation as to why you appeared out of nowhere in the gardens *behind* our home."

Aristotle walked forward and gave Alexander a big hug. "Of course, my boy. Of course. We'll explain everything." He took a step back, his hands still gripping the shoulders of his student. "But I just can't tell you how happy I am to see you alive and well. My heart is soaring."

Sera understood why he was showing so much emotion. Just an hour earlier he'd been told his most famous pupil had been killed, and yet here he stood now, safe and sound.

Alexander himself, of course, didn't quite get it. "I just visited with you a month ago. And there's not much around here that could hurt me besides some garden tools. Save your worries, master, for the day I go to battle with my father, the hegemon."

When he spoke, Alexander had a grandness about him that impressed Sera. Even though he looked young, there was just something . . . *majestic* about him.

"Um, excuse me?"

Sera and everyone else looked at Dak, still hanging from the statue.

"The dogs are gone," Riq said. "Is there a reason you're still hanging up there like an ugly tree ornament?"

"Yes, actually. It was easy to get up here with dogs trying to bite me, but I'm not sure how to get back down. And as much as I love Plato . . ."

Riq and Sera stepped forward and provided footholds and balance as Dak climbed to the ground. Then the boy smoothed his clothes and heaved a big sigh.

"Tough work running from man-eating beasts," he said. "You guys should try it sometime."

They all stood silent for a moment, awkwardness hanging in the air like drapes. Then Aristotle finally broke the ice.

"Introductions!" he exclaimed, a little too excitedly. He cleared his throat, then proceeded to tell who was who, and of course Dak shook Alexander's hand when it came to be his turn.

"I've always wanted to meet you," Dak said. "Even though I didn't honestly know a lot about you until the Hyst—"

"Very good, very good," Aristotle interrupted. "Now that we're all friends, let us retire to the palace and get comfortable. Alex, I don't think I need to tell you that there's a lot to talk about."

The young man nodded, then finally sheathed his sword. "Yes, sounds like a fine plan, master. But I must warn you . . ."

"About what?" the philosopher prodded.

Alexander took a second to look at the people he'd just met. "I don't think my mother is going to be very happy to see you."

∞

As pretty as the outside of Olympias's palace was, the inside took Sera's breath away. Alexander's mother—or her decorator—had an obvious taste for the international. There was pottery from Egypt, rugs from Persia, bronze statues from Italy, furniture of all sizes and shapes, not one piece looking like it came from the same place as another. Sera wished she could transport the entire house into the future — she'd love to live in a place with so much variety and personality.

As for Olympias herself, she was as glamorous and beautiful as her palace.

Black hair hung to her waist, with ribbons and chains of silver and gold interwoven in intricate designs throughout. Her gown seemed to glow, white and shiny, which brought out her flawless olive skin and blazing green eyes. The amethyst mentioned earlier hung in the hollow of her neck. She even had perfect teeth, and Sera had the thought that it should be against some universal law for people to look so good.

"I did not invite you here," she said to Aristotle after Alexander introduced them all to her. They were sitting in some kind of fancy parlor, with cushion-laden wooden furniture and colorful tapestries hanging on the walls. One huge window let in a burst of golden sunlight. Olympias was the only one standing, towering like the statue of Plato outside.

"No, you did not," Aristotle said, surprisingly firm after the diss. "But I assure you we have vital reasons for being here. We only need a few moments of your time to explain."

Not so much as a muscle twitched on the face of Olympias. "Time that I do not have."

The philosopher finally stood to put himself on the

same level as their hostess. "I would expect better treatment after all I've done for your son, my lady. I've come to learn of a threat that poses great danger to that very boy." He glanced at Alexander, who sat quietly in a chair located in the corner of the room—he seemed to be analyzing every word, every movement, content to wait for more information. "I highly recommend you take a seat and hear us out."

Olympias eyed the man, not moving for what seemed to Sera like a full hour. But then she finally smiled, acting as if she'd been doing so since the moment they met. After a brief nod of her head, she took a seat in the biggest chair in the room, one that was draped in silk and appeared to be made out of solid gold. She looked for all the world like a queen on her throne.

"Very well," she said in a stately manner. Then her eyes found a spot on a couch, right next to Sera. "Please, sit." Somehow she'd turned things around to make Aristotle seem like the obstinate one.

But the philosopher was unfazed. He plopped down ungracefully and started talking. "We've uncovered an assassination plot."

For the first time, the lady's demeanor broke a little—eyes widened in shock, a little tremor in her mouth. And Sera knew why. She probably thought Aristotle was talking about her plan to have King Philip murdered. But she recovered and waited to hear more.

"Someone wants your son dead, Olympias," Aristotle continued. "And I can't tell you why or how we know, but we do, and we know that she is coming here to do it. We must work together to prevent it from happening."

"And why should I believe you?" Olympias responded. Sera wanted to growl like the dogs earlier — she really didn't like this woman.

"Because you trusted me for years to tutor your son and raise him in the ways of wisdom and light. If you doubt me, or refuse to protect him, then I'd have to conclude that you have your own ill tidings planned for the very near future."

The tension in the room was strung as tightly as a piano wire. Sera held her breath.

Olympias waited. And waited. And waited. She had the patience of a crocodile. Finally, she answered, and Sera didn't know if she would ever breathe again when she heard the words.

"You must be talking about my new friend. The woman named Tilda."

Lesson Learned

DAK WANTED to stand up, scream and yell, demand answers. But he was so stunned by what Olympias had said that he just sat there, staring at her. The others reacted the same. Alexander's mother knew she'd gotten them good.

"She told me this might happen," Olympias continued when no one questioned her statement. "We've been meeting at the market, and she's become a very good friend. She's so . . . different, with that red hair that shines in the sun like fired iron. I can hardly wait for our meetings. In fact, I've invited her to come and meet Alexander soon. It's not often I allow guests into my home."

Dak closed his eyes for a second and shook his head. *What in the world was going on here?*

Alexander spoke next from his chair in the corner. "Would someone please explain this nonsense? My teacher says that someone plans to kill me, and then my mother says her new market friend told her this would happen. Explain."

Dak looked at him in awe. The heir to the hegemon sat with his ankles casually crossed, leaning back, and yet he radiated a sense of command. It even seemed to affect his mom. She stammered a bit and then did her best to answer.

"Tilda is a wonderful, sweet, compassionate person, my son. She told me the entire story of how these . . . children"—she gave a very nasty glare to each one of them—"had escaped their homes and fled to our land, bent on causing trouble. I won't bore you with the details, but suffice it to say that they have a vendetta against my beautiful friend, and she told me they'd come here, saying wicked things about her. Her wisdom and foresight is evident."

Dak couldn't take another second of this ridiculousness. "She's brainwashed you! That's what she does. All nice and sweet until she stabs you in the back. Ever think there's an actual *reason* we'd come here to say bad things about her? If she's so perfect, why would she have to *warn* you that we'd . . . warn you about her?" Dak groaned. He was sounding like an idiot.

Sera seemed to agree, shooting him her special look. "What my friend's trying to say is that this woman, Tilda, is really good at convincing people to do what she says. She's the leader of a . . . group that's very . . . evil." It was her turn to groan.

Dak hid his smile. At least he wasn't alone on the idiot train.

Olympias stood, folded her arms, and took a few steps

forward. "I think I've lived long enough, seen enough, met enough people to be able to take care of myself. I know when a soul is good, and when a soul is . . . what was the word you used?" She looked at Sera. "Evil, I believe. Yes, I know. Trust me, I know very well. . . ." She trailed off with that last part, her gaze going distant, and Dak knew she was thinking of King Philip. The man who'd broken her heart and stood in the way of her son's ascendance.

"Olympias, please." Aristotle used a soft voice. "Please listen to us. Please trust us. I spent a good part of my life teaching your son—preparing him for a great future. I couldn't bear it if he were to lose his life. Alex is in danger, and I firmly believe that it's all because of this woman. This . . . Tilda."

"I'll be the judge of that," she responded. "I'm well protected anyway. When she comes here, if I sense any—"

"Mother!" Alexander shouted. He jolted from his chair and practically charged to where she stood—Dak thought for a split second he might tackle her like a rogue linebacker. But he stopped in front of her and grabbed her by the shoulders. "Did you tell this woman where we live? Where our home is? Did you?"

Olympias appeared shocked by the outburst, eyes wide, leaning back from her son. She finally nodded timidly, and Dak wondered if maybe she was snapping out of her brainwashed delusion of Tilda.

Alexander pulled her into a hug, then kissed her on the cheek. "I love you, Mama, but I would fall backward off the tallest ship into a sea of sharks if my teacher told me to. I trust him with my life, heart, and soul. You should not have done this thing. You shouldn't have told her where we live."

"You trust *him* more than me?" she replied, her expression showing pure heartbreak.

"It's not the Olympiad. It's not a race. I trust you both."

Besides the sweet glorious glee of hearing Alexander actually mention the Olympics—which originated in his country long before they renewed it in the modern day—Dak felt unsettled. Things just didn't seem to be going well, or the way he expected. Tilda was too smart.

He noticed Aristotle was looking at him.

"Any suggestions?" the man asked him.

Dak wished he had that moment on video. Aristotle asking him for advice.

"I say we lock Alexander in a closet and have his guards and dogs right outside the door for a week." It'd never happen, but Dak didn't know how else to make sure—absolutely sure—that Tilda couldn't get to him.

Alex pulled out his sword and pointed it at Dak. "Remember the lesson you were supposed to learn on that statue? Do I look like the kind of person who'd allow someone to lock me in a closet?"

Dak shook his head, liking this guy more by the minute.

"That's a good student." He sheathed his sword. "Now, come. We're going to the market to hunt down this woman that everyone seems to think wants me dead. She has her own lesson to learn."

Without waiting for a response — as if he expected any human who ever crossed his path in life to obey his commands without question — Alexander walked out of the room. Dak followed happily at his heels.

16

Visitor

RIQ FELL in line with everyone else as they marched through the grand halls of the palace and out the front door, finally walking down huge marble steps onto a wide lawn. It spread out like a green sea before them, and Alexander didn't hesitate a second as he stomped onto it and kept moving, his muscles clenched as if he wanted to run instead.

The two guards who'd accompanied him earlier had appeared, hurrying to get right behind him. Then came Aristotle, walking with confident strides. Next was Olympias, having lost every ounce of the stately, towering demeanor she'd shown earlier.

After them, Riq, Sera, and Dak tried to keep up, side by side, Sera in the middle.

Riq leaned in toward her. "You think she'll be there?"

"I don't know," Sera said with a shrug. "But since we've probably already altered what she originally intended to do, we need to stay close to Alexander."

Dak made a scoffing sound. "Like we can do anything

to protect him. Look at that dude. He could take down three bears with his pinkie."

"Did you lose your brain somewhere?" Sera responded. "We just found out that Tilda killed him."

"Yeah, but she probably sneaked up on him or something. Now that we warned him, I bet he'll be fine. Man, for all we know, we've already fixed the Prime Break. Holy cow. What if that's true?"

Riq had only been half listening, seeing movement up ahead, beyond where the huge lawn met a road. A group of people, maybe. But what Dak said really struck him. The kid could be right. Totally right. His heart lifted a little.

Then he got a better glimpse of what lay ahead. "Who are those guys up there?" he asked. There seemed to be twenty or thirty people, and they'd just left the road and walked onto the vast lawn surrounding Olympias's palace.

"I don't know," Sera responded, "but they don't . . ." Her voice trailed off and she stopped walking.

So did Riq. "What?" he asked. But the word had barely left his mouth when he saw *exactly* what. Behind the others coming toward them—at a brisk pace, body language screaming that they weren't on a nice, casual stroll—a woman strode along, mostly hidden from view because she was shorter than the others. But every once in a while Riq caught a glimpse of flaming red hair.

"Wait!" Dak called out to Alexander and the guards. Aristotle and Olympias had already stopped. "Tilda's up there!"

Alex turned around, not a trace of sweat or deep breathing to show that he'd practically been running down the lawn. He looked at his teacher. "That's the woman you came to warn me about?" Then his eyes moved to his mom. "That's your new friend from the market?"

Both of them simply nodded.

Alexander pulled the sword from its sheath and his two guards followed his lead; the scrape of metal sliding against hard leather rang through the air like birdsong.

"And your friend needed an escort of twenty soldiers to come say hello?" Alex asked.

Riq was watching the oncoming crowd, and the heir to the hegemon was right. Those marching toward them, protecting Tilda in a semicircle as they walked, were dressed and armed just like Alex and his guards. The glint of breastplates and helms and drawn daggers, swords, and spears sparkled in the sunlight, some of the flashes almost blinding.

Olympias had gone totally pale, every bit of her seeming like she'd aged ten years in a minute, her eyes hard with worry. "I don't understand. I . . . things have gotten so complicated."

It doesn't matter, Riq thought. They were here, and Riq and his friends were ridiculously outnumbered. The front line of soldiers stopped about thirty feet from where Alexander stood, but Tilda kept walking until she slipped past the armed men and finally stood where Riq could see her head to toe.

Below that fiery hair, her black lips made the rest

of her skin look ghostly white. She wore tight-fitting clothes, bloodred and charcoal gray, that looked totally out of place compared to everyone else. Her face bore no expression whatsoever. In her right hand, she gripped an infinity-shaped device made out of gleaming metal.

The Eternity Ring.

"Hello, Olympias," Tilda said, her voice so soft and smooth that it almost convinced Riq she was genuine. For a split second, he felt the outrageous urge to hear her out. There was something magnetic about her, like the woman had evil spells to hypnotize and manipulate whomever she wanted. "It's good to see you again so soon. Thanks again for the invitation to visit your beautiful home. I can tell it's quite the keeper."

"You always bring along a bunch of hired thugs for friendly get-togethers?" Riq asked, his heart rate ticking up. He was surprised that Tilda appeared to have a translation device as advanced as that of the Hystorians. The SQ probably stole *that* technology from them, too.

Tilda was shaking her head, taking looks back at the soldiers she'd brought with her. "I'm done taking chances, as you can see. This isn't the first time I've come back in time to do the job that the SQ *needs* to be done." She faltered a bit on the last couple of words—almost slurring them—and took a step to the left as if she'd suddenly lost her balance. "I hired every sword I could find in the city, and came to meet you here, exactly where I knew you would be."

She pointed somewhere over Riq's shoulder, and he

turned to look. About fifty feet away, a woman was standing beside a tree, staring at them. Impossibly, it was Tilda — another version of Tilda, holding the Eternity Ring. A couple of seconds later, she activated the device and warped away in a blur of light and sound. Everyone gasped in surprise.

Riq spun around and shouted at the Tilda who was still there. "Are you crazy?"

"You can't mess with time like that!" Sera added. "No wonder you can barely stand. Jumping around with the Ring like that is going to fry your brain — not to mention do who-knows-what to reality itself!"

Dak was still staring back at the spot where the other Tilda had disappeared. Aristotle, Olympias, Alexander — even Tilda's own allies — just stood there, wondering what in the heck was going on.

Tilda stumbled again, but then moved a few steps forward as if she'd meant to do it. "Say what you want. Pretend to have all the high and mighty ideals you want. But I'm telling you, the Hystorians *do not* understand what's at stake. We can all fight here, and lose a lot of lives in the process. But if you would just *listen* to me . . ." Her face scrunched up in genuine frustration, and Riq found a small part of himself wanted to give her the benefit of the doubt again.

"I don't know you," Aristotle said, his voice deeper and holding more resonance than Riq had heard in him yet. "And I don't know the smallest part of what lies in the future or the extent of this battle between your . . .

SQ and the Hystorians. But I do know that talking things through — trying to come to an understanding, might be our wisest course of action for right now."

Maybe because we're outnumbered three to one, Riq thought darkly.

Tilda took a few steps forward, and her focus was on Dak, Sera, and Riq, not the others in the group. "I know you think we've done bad things. Horrible things. But I'm telling you, we're not idiots. We're not *evil*. In fact, I know something that you don't — that *none* of the Hystorians know."

"And what's that?" Riq asked.

Tilda answered quietly, her face a mask of stone. "How to stop the Cataclysm."

17

Council of Friends

SERA FELT a tingle in her temples, as if there were static electricity prickling her skin. She had encountered Tilda before, and it was never a pleasant experience. But this time felt different. Tilda herself *seemed* different. Desperate. Sera couldn't shake the feeling that the woman was more dangerous than ever.

"You have no idea how to stop the Cataclysm," Dak said. "The SQ boneheads are the ones who've been trying to make sure it happens!" The volume of his voice had risen with every word.

Tilda laughed as if she'd heard something horrible, not funny. When she did, she also winced like something hurt. Sera understood. Too much warping through time and your body started to feel like it had been stretched on a medieval torture device.

"Make sure it happens?" the woman said after she recovered. "You kids are supposed to be smart. You have to be, or the Hystorians would never have let you go back in time to fix their so-called Great Breaks." She paused, taking a second to look all three of them in the eyes. Alexander and everyone else seemed content to observe for the moment. "You are intelligent, right? Or am I wrong?"

"Of course we're smart," Sera snapped. "What's your point?"

Tilda held up a finger. "This. This is my point. Why on earth would we spend our entire effort—sacrificing lives and time and immense amounts of money—to run an organization that wants the world to end? What would be the point? If we want to rule humanity, don't you think we'd want there to be a place for them to *live*? It's insane to think we want the Cataclysm to happen. It's outrageous and most definitely *not* intelligent."

Sera wanted to say something, rebuke her somehow. But any potential words froze on her tongue. As much as she hated to admit it, the woman had made a good point.

Tilda seemed to sense a victory in their silence. "Our ways have been tough, I'll be the first to admit it. We've been harsh because we have to be. Yes, we've ruled with an iron fist, and we've done everything in our power to make sure this man"—she tipped her head toward Aristotle—"didn't fulfill his plan to mess up the world. To drive it toward the very Cataclysm that you think you're preventing."

She paused, and pinched the bridge of her nose as she took a deep breath. "Time and space are fine. The fabric of reality is fine. What you're doing—messing with the past, trying to change major events—that's the thing that will drive us to destruction. This young man . . ."

Tilda paused and turned a sad gaze on Alexander. "He dies. He *must* die, for the good of the world. Whether by Pausanius's hand or my own. I'm here to convince you to let that happen. With words, if possible. If not . . ."

She didn't need to say the rest. Sera swallowed, feeling uncertain about their mission for the first time. Aristotle was the founder of the whole order of Hystorians — but was it possible that he'd created the organization for selfish reasons? That he simply couldn't bear to see his favorite student killed? That it wasn't about the fabric of time, but about a softhearted man who wanted to save a boy who could have been great? Sera hated it, hated this wave of doubt. "But why all the natural disasters?" she asked Tilda. "You've seen the state of the world. Plus, I went to the future and I saw the Cataclysm for myself. In a world that the SQ has been running, by the way."

"Exactly," the woman replied. "You saw it. You went to the future *after* correcting some of the Hystorians' so-called Breaks. You saw a catastrophic future that *you* created. Again, you're smart. Think about these things, and you'll see that I'm right."

Aristotle turned away from Tilda and walked to stand with Sera and her friends. Alexander, his guards, and Olympias did as well. They stood in a circle, their job now to decide the fate of the entire world. Maybe the universe. *No biggie,* Sera thought.

"I don't trust this woman," Alexander said. He still held his sword as if he wanted to strike the first person to disagree with him.

"Amen," Dak added. "I don't trust that lady any farther than Riq can throw Sera."

Riq's face wrinkled up in confusion for a second, but then he just shrugged. "She's a trickster. Whatever she says we should do, I'm doing the opposite."

Sera looked at Olympias, but the woman was silent, deep in thought.

Aristotle scratched his long beard and sighed heavily. Then he spoke.

"This woman believes what she's saying. Of that, I have no doubt. But there's also a . . . darkness about her. Not to mention the simple fact that she marched twenty armed men down here to kill the boy I spent years training to be a great king someday. And I feel the goodness in each of you." He stepped forward and took a second to touch Dak, Sera, then Riq on the shoulder.

"I don't even see a question, to be honest," the philosopher said. "There's no way in Hades or the halls of Zeus that I'll let that woman take the life of Alexander."

"He is the *son* of Zeus," Olympias whispered distantly.

"I don't need your help," the young heir said, his eyes slightly moist. "But I appreciate the offer."

Fear crawled like a caterpillar up Sera's spine. They only had three soldiers, and Tilda had twenty.

"What are you thinking?" Dak whispered to her.

She shrugged. "I just don't know what we're going to do."

Dak turned to Alexander. "Can you call more of your friends? It looks like we have pretty bad odds."

Alex spun the sword in his hand. "Today you will learn the greatness of Alexander" was all he said, but it came out sounding like something that should be engraved on a plaque. The young man turned toward Tilda and stepped away from the circle of friends they'd formed, heading straight toward the woman.

"My lady!" he yelled out. "We have counseled with my teacher and master, the wisest man who has ever graced this world. And our decision was an easy one. We reject your foul proposal and order you to leave the lands of my mother, Olympias of Epirus, daughter of King Neoptolemus. Leave, or the punishment will be severe."

"So be it." Tilda nodded, then took slow and steady steps backward, her eyes never leaving Alexander. The soldiers she'd hired parted to let her pass, and soon all of them were once again in front of her, a shield of armed and angry men.

"Kill them," she said, as calmly as the most seasoned battle commander.

"But, Tilda!" Olympias screamed, finally coming alive. "You were my friend! We were like sisters!"

Tilda frowned. "Be sure and kill her, too."

18

A Dance on the Grass

ANY EMPATHY or understanding Riq had felt for Tilda vanished as quickly as a drop of water thrown into a fire. He almost sensed it leave his mind, like a tangible thing. The woman had been doing her best to brainwash them, but the spell was finally broken.

The soldiers she'd brought along started marching forward, drawing swords and daggers and spears. Their walk turned into a trot, then a run. Roaring battle yells, they charged in to do as their master had ordered.

A cold rush of terror washed through Riq, knowing they had absolutely no chance of fighting against all those muscles and weapons. Unless somehow they could wrestle a couple of the soldiers down, maybe steal their weapons . . .

He looked at Sera, and his heart hurt to see how scared she was. Dak, too. It was up to him, then. He would gladly sacrifice himself to ensure all they'd fought for wasn't lost now, with victory so close.

He took a step forward, but Sera grabbed his arm. "What are you doing?" she hissed.

"Hold," Alexander suddenly said. Riq had been focused on Tilda's group, but now he saw that Alex and his two guards had formed a line, swords drawn, their bodies rigid in a fighting stance.

"Hold," the future king repeated, louder because the small army of soldiers was almost on them, screaming and yelling and clanging their weapons, feet pounding the ground like horses' hooves.

"Hold!" Alex shouted again, a thundercrack of sound that overwhelmed everything else. The charging army was only fifteen feet away. *"NOW!"*

Riq actually jumped at the boom of the last word, its echo bouncing off the shields of the soldiers as if they were cliff walls. And then he witnessed a flurry of movement and speed that he hadn't known possible.

Alex and his guards swept forward in a burst, their swords swinging through the air as if powered by great machines, cutting and slashing. Their free hands held daggers, which jabbed and stabbed in unsuspected places, felling their foes as surely as the huge blades. One by one, Tilda's soldiers fell to the ground, writhing in agony, bleeding, screaming. Alexander in particular was like a tornado of human flesh, his movements a blur, his feet dancing, his sword flashing in the sun as it cut down one man after another.

Riq watched, stunned, caught between surprise and wanting to jump up and down to cheer their hero. Dak had no reservations. He was cheering, pumping his fists as he did so.

Olympias had a huge smile on her face, beaming with pride. She turned to the others and spoke over the sounds of clashing battle. "He's the greatest soldier to ever live. Someday he'll make a great king. I've given my whole life to making sure that happens."

That last part gave Riq the chills because he knew exactly what she had up her sleeve to ensure Alexander became the hegemon sooner than later.

"Guys, look!" Sera shouted, pointing beyond where Alexander and his two buddies were slowly but surely winning their small war.

Riq did as she said, and saw Tilda running. She had the Eternity Ring gripped in her hands and was sprinting all out for a thicker grouping of trees on the edge of the huge lawn.

"Not this time," Riq said, mostly to himself, already on the run to skirt around the soldiers and pursue Tilda. He was *not* going to let her get away. "Come on! Before she warps again." He was surprised she hadn't preprogrammed the thing already, just in case. It showed how overly confident she'd been that victory was in hand.

Dak and Sera stayed on his heels — he could hear them breathing but he didn't dare take the time to look. Riq watched his step and watched Tilda, taking as direct a course as possible without risking a sword chopping off his head.

Tilda reached the trees and disappeared behind a huge oak, just as Riq cleared the last soldier and started sprinting across the expanse of grass. He sucked in each breath and spit it back out, his chest heaving with exertion. It had been a while since he'd run so hard. They were so close to victory. *So close.* And he just knew that if Tilda got away again, she could ruin everything.

"Hurry!" Dak yelled from behind him.

"What do you think I'm doing?!" Riq shouted right back, though he could barely get the words out.

He reached the trees and didn't slow, bursting into the relative darkness of the shade. Whipping his head back and forth, he searched for where she'd gone, terrified that she'd already whisked away into a wormhole. Riq finally slowed, knowing he couldn't risk passing her by, and Dak ran into him, knocking both of them to the ground. Riq grunted and struggled to get back to his feet, pushing Dak off of him.

"Over there!" Sera yelled, pointing.

Riq didn't pause to ask questions, pushing off the ground and exploding in that direction like a runner off the blocks. He rounded a tree and saw her, kneeling on the ground, furiously working at the controls of her Eternity Ring. Riq ran, going faster than he'd ever thought possible. Tilda looked up at him, her face fraught with worry, tensed and tightly pulled over her skull. He saw her hand moving toward the final button, the one that would take her away.

"NO!" he screamed, diving into the air.

His shoulders slammed into Tilda's body, knocking the Ring out of her hands. Out of the corner of his eye he saw it land and bounce, finally coming to a rest in a big pile of leaves. He and Tilda rolled, one on top of the other, about three times before they, too, came to a stop.

"Get off of me!" she yelled. "Get *off*!"

Surprisingly strong, she was able to push him away. Riq quickly got to his feet to run after the Eternity Ring, but Sera had already snatched it up in her hands. She held it close to her body, cradling it with both arms. Dak stood next to her, and both of them looked like they'd been underwater for five minutes by the way they were breathing so heavily.

Riq turned to Tilda again just in time for her to slap him across the face. It stung, made him stumble backward.

"How dare you!" she screamed at him, her eyes burning with hatred. "You brats have no idea what you're doing! No idea! If you had half the vision that my people and I do, you'd grab a dagger right now and go stab Alexander in the heart!"

Riq didn't respond. Neither did Dak or Sera. They stared at the woman, seeing the insanity that barely kept itself hidden beneath her exterior. She was cracking, cracking for good. Riq knew without the slightest doubt that Tilda could never be trusted with the Eternity Ring.

"Give it back to me," she said in an almost scary, calm voice to Sera. "Hand it over, nice and easy, and I promise the SQ will leave your parents alone."

Sera let out a little gasp, and Riq knew the woman's words had hurt his friend. And just like that, he hated Tilda a little bit more. And made his decision.

Walking up to Sera, he held out his hand. "I know what to do."

She hesitated a second, and Riq could see the doubt in her eyes. Tilda had almost gotten to her. But she came to her senses, giving him a grim nod and handing over the device. He felt its cool, smooth surface, could sense the outrageous amount of power contained within its infinity-shaped shell. Turning back to Tilda, he said, "You could've done so much good for the world."

Then he gripped one end of the device, reached back, and slammed it into the trunk of the closest tree.

"STOP!" screamed Tilda. *"STOP!"*

But Riq didn't stop. He hit the tree with it again. And again. And again. With all his strength, throwing his hatred for the woman into every single strike, he pummeled the trunk over and over, until he heard a crack, then a bigger crack, then a metallic splintering, followed by more cracks.

Finally, on one last heave, the Eternity Ring exploded into a mess of broken fragments, falling to the ground in a rain of sharp debris. All the while, Tilda wailed like a lost child.

19

Just Walk Away

DAK HAD mixed feelings as he watched Riq go crazy-town with the Eternity Ring, smashing the thing into tiny bits. On the one hand, he relished the painful cries coming from Tilda — the woman deserved what she was getting — but on the other hand, destroying such a valuable piece of technology might not be the smartest thing his friend had ever done. But in terms of showmanship, the guy got an A-plus.

When Riq was finally done, letting the last little piece of metal shard drop from his hand, he took a step backward and stared along with the rest of them at the ruins of the Ring. Tilda's haunted screams had faded into more of a hitching series of sobs. Dak almost felt sorry for her, but then remembered what a master of manipulation she'd proven to be.

Riq looked a little embarrassed for what he'd done, but Dak wanted to high-five him, though that seemed slightly inappropriate for the moment. Instead, he walked over and lightly patted him on the back.

"You did the right thing," he whispered. "She brought it on herself."

Sera was right next to them, and agreed. "Let's go back. She can't hurt anybody anymore. The Eternity Ring's destroyed and she probably spent every last penny hiring all those soldiers. Come on."

Riq eyed Tilda, who seemed to be in total shock, still staring at the smashed parts of the Ring as she cried. "How can we just leave her? Who knows what kind of trouble she can stir up? She's *Tilda*, man."

"What're we going to do?" Sera replied. "Kill her? Throw her in jail?"

"Maybe in the opposite order," Dak said, hoping a laugh could relax everybody a bit. But instead he got two cold looks in response. "I don't know. Aristotle can figure out what to do with her."

"You're right," Sera said. "It's not really our place. We've done enough damage making sure she's stuck here forever. Let's go back and check on Alexander."

Riq muttered something that Dak couldn't hear, then stormed off through the trees in the direction of the lawn. Sera followed, and Dak had taken one step when he heard Tilda say something from behind him.

"You'll regret this," she said, her voice barely above a whisper.

"Oh, please," he responded. "Leave it alone, Tilda. Aren't things bad enough?"

She didn't respond. She only turned from him and walked away.

∞

Quite the sight awaited Dak when he caught up with Sera and Riq. Every last soldier that had come at Tilda's command to kill Alexander either lay on the ground with nasty wounds, some of them dead and unmoving, or knelt on the ground, their hands tied behind their backs. Swords and daggers and clubs, smeared with blood, littered the green canvas of the lawn.

Alexander stood by Aristotle, surveying the scene, while Olympias was gone, maybe to call help to clean up, arrest people, whatever needed to be done.

The philosopher seemed quite relieved to see that Dak and the others had survived their own little mission — the relief on the man's face made Dak feel happy from top to bottom.

"Do you think we've done it?" Aristotle asked them after congratulations and explanations were done. "Have we saved Alexander, prevented the Prime Break you told me about?"

Dak was at a loss for words. The man seemed to think they had all the answers, and he guessed it made sense since they were from the future and all. But he was the dude who started the Hystorians. Deep down, Dak was hoping the guy would tell them "You've done it! All is right in the world! The Cataclysm is no more! Let's party!" Instead he was asking *them* for reassurance.

After an awkward silence, Sera finally answered. "Honestly, I don't think we know. Things haven't happened like we expected. I mean, we were *supposed* to save Alexander from a guy named Pausanius, out in the army camps of his dad."

"Pausanius?" Alexander repeated, his tone harsh. He'd been cleaning his sword, but he was now all ears, his body rigid with attention. "The nobleman? The man who's been serving as one of my father's bodyguards?"

Sera stammered to answer, but nothing coherent came out. Dak took over since he was the one who knew the history the best.

"That's him," he said. "I know it can't be good to hear, but your mom hired that guy to kill King Philip so that you could become the king sooner rather than later. She didn't want him to kill you, of course, but you showed up and . . . Well, you know how things go sometimes. Bada-boom bada-bing, and you died, too."

Riq gave him a sharp look. "Seriously? What a way with words you have."

"I'm just telling him how it is. Or was. Or whatever." He faced Alexander again, whose face had grown about five shades of red darker. "But then Tilda started jumping around time and changed everything up. We had to come back here and save you, and now that you know what's going on, you'll be safe, right?" He hated to think Riq was right, but Dak didn't feel like a single word popping out of his mouth had made a lick of sense.

Alexander didn't look well. He stared at the ground, his eyes afire, his face growing even redder. And his chest heaved with breaths.

"Alex?" Aristotle asked. "What's wrong? We've made

things right, and there's still plenty of time to stop your mother from her ill-fated plan. Just let me handle her, okay?"

But Alexander wasn't listening. He backed away, still not looking anybody in the eye, shaking his head, fuming with anger. Olympias appeared then, with a host of servants and guards to start the clean-up process. When Alexander saw her, he went ballistic.

"How could you?" he screamed, the words ragged as they tore from his throat. "How could you do this thing?" And then he was running toward the stables, not listening to anyone who tried to get him to come back.

Dak looked at his friends, then back at Aristotle. Everyone seemed frozen to the ground, stunned, unsure of what to do. Olympias marched toward them, pulling up in front of the philosopher, furious.

"Why?" she spat at him. "Why are you meddling so much? *I* know what's best for my son and his future. Only me! I want you to leave here at once!"

The philosopher was unfazed. "You have to stop this nonsense, Olympias. Let matters follow their own course now."

"Philip will die!" she yelled, not a trace of her dazzling self left from when Dak had first met her. She shook, and her skin was an unnatural color of rage. "My son must be the hegemon and lead the world to glory!"

Before Aristotle could reply, a horse came leaping from the stables, breaking into a gallop that tore up the grass of the lawn. Alexander was on top, reins in hands, leaning forward.

"Alex!" Aristotle yelled. "What are you doing on Bucephalus?"

Bucephalus, Dak thought. *What a weird name for a horse.*

The heir to the king didn't slow, certainly didn't stop. But Dak heard him answer as animal and rider flew past them.

"I'm going to save the king."

Dak's insides melted. That's how the whole mess happened in the first place. It appeared the Prime Break was still in play after all.

2 0

The Crumpled Scroll

IN THE next few minutes there was a lot of yelling. A lot of arguing. Also a lot of standing around looking at one another with blank faces. Riq watched it all in silence.

Aristotle scolded Olympias. She scolded him right back. Dak and Sera tried to convince a whole host of different people to get on horses and chase Alexander down, force him to come back before he got himself killed just the way the original history played out. No one seemed too keen on that idea. It was like telling a zebra to go talk a pride of lions away from fresh meat.

As for Riq, he was lost on the inside. It had felt so good to lose himself to his anger. Now that it was gone, he felt empty. The truth was that he liked having an enemy to focus on. Tilda had been the source of so much fear and fury and anxiety in his life. And now she was defeated, pathetic, and Riq was left with fears that weren't so easy to punch or kick or bite.

He rubbed his hands together, wiping away the last droplets of fuel from the Eternity Ring.

Suddenly Sera was standing before him. She touched his elbow and spoke low, out of earshot of Dak. "Riq, what was that all about back there?"

Riq grimaced. "Sorry," he said. "I guess I overdid it a little."

Sera shook her head. "Tilda had that coming to her, and worse. I mean before. You were ready to jump right into the fight with twenty heavily armed men."

"Sera," he began. Then he paused, searching for the words. "You know this is it for me. I can't risk going back to the future when we're done here. The mission—"

"The mission is important," Sera cut in. "But so are you." She gave him a look that was somehow friendly and dangerous at the same time. "Ever since 1850, you've been way too willing to sacrifice yourself for the mission. You've thrown yourself in front of swords, spears, and bombs. It's got to stop, Riq. Even if you really can't come back to the future, that doesn't mean you can't have a future of your own."

Riq blinked mutely, unsure what to say to that. Had he really been that careless? Had he been acting like a hero or a lunatic with a death wish?

"You two want to join us?" Dak hollered. "We need to make a decision."

"Well, you won't do it in my home," Olympias announced. She'd recovered some of her earlier hauteur, and once again looked like a princess. "Aristotle, you've done great things for my family, but you were also paid in kind. You're no longer welcome here." She raised a hand when he started to protest. "No. Please. Enough quarrels for one day. Please respect my wishes and leave. Immediately."

"Respect?" Dak blurted. "You wanna talk about respect? Not only are you planning on killing the king, you know now that it could very well mean your kid dies, too. And you're not going to do anything? What kind of person are you anyway?"

Sera touched Dak on the arm, her eyes down. Riq felt for him, but he also knew there was nothing they could do to change things through Olympias.

"Hey," Riq said to his friend. "Dude. Just let it go. Come on."

"Yes," Aristotle agreed. "It's plain that dealing with this woman can no longer lead to solutions. Dak. Sera. Riq. Let's go and gather our thoughts in a place more welcoming than here."

They started to walk off, and Olympias called out some parting words.

"Never come back."

∞

They found a little alcove in an abandoned warehouse, where the smell of fish and salt and rotting meat mixed with the scent of flowers that covered the grounds nearby. It all combined into something that wasn't altogether unpleasant, and for some reason it made Sera's stomach rumble with hunger. They sat on old benches of stone — cracked and dirty — and tried to figure out what they should do next.

"Look on the bright side," Dak said. "We're no worse off than before. Actually, we're better off in some ways. We still have to stop this Pausanius dude from killing Alexander, which was right where we started. But at least we know that Tilda is out of the picture. Right?"

Sera didn't think that was much to get excited about. "Yeah, I guess. But now Olympias can warn her man, make sure he's more careful."

"But," Riq said, "that might be good, too. She obviously doesn't really want to kill her son. Maybe she'll drive that through the guy's head: *Don't kill Alexander, no matter what.*"

Aristotle was shaking his head. "All excellent points, but I fear you're missing the most important. Whether or not Pausanius means him any harm, Alexander is now out for the man's blood. If Alexander defends his father, or avenges him, Pausanius will fight back to protect his own life."

Dak scoffed at that. "Did you see the way he mowed down all those soldiers out there? Unless this Pausanius guy is Hercules or something, I think old boy Alex will be just fine."

"Except he wasn't." Sera didn't mean to be flippant, but it was the sad truth that Pausanius had killed Alexander, no matter how great a fighter the heir to Philip might have been. "He died, and there's nothing to say it won't happen just like it did in our history books."

Dak opened his mouth for a retort, but then left it hanging there. She was right, and he knew it.

"So, what do we do?" Riq asked.

Aristotle gave the answer. "It's quite simple, really. We use your time device to jump ahead a few days to the future, traveling to the camps of King Philip. Once there, we do everything in our power to keep Pausanius away from the hegemon and his son. I still have a lot of sway, I believe."

Sera liked to hear him sound so confident. "Perfect. That's about the best plan we can hope for. I just hope they believe us."

Before anyone could respond to her, a soldier appeared from around the corner, collapsing in a heap right in front of their benches. He was ragged and bruised and bloody, gasping for each and every breath as if his lungs had been punctured. Sera recognized him as one of Tilda's men. She jumped up in fear but then realized just how weak the man was, not a threat at all. Everyone else had stood up as well.

"Aris . . . totle," the man wheezed.

The philosopher knelt down by the man, though keeping his distance in case it was a trap. "Yes. What is it?"

"You . . . spared . . . my life." The man's face pinched up in pain, and he took several long, struggling breaths. "I want to . . . repay you." He reached out and opened his hand, where a scroll had been clutched between his fingers.

Aristotle stood up, took the scroll, unrolled it, then read through it quickly. When he was finished, he looked right at Dak.

"When you told me your story, you mentioned something about your parents possibly being in this time period, correct?"

Dak nodded uncertainly. "Yeah, what's going on?"

"They have the name Smyth, just like yours?"

"Yes!"

The philosopher's face creased in concern. "An unusual name for these parts, so I can't imagine it to be a coincidence."

This time it was Sera's turn to yell in frustration, Aristotle or not. "Tell us!"

The man complied. "It looks like your Tilda gave us one last blow. If I understand correctly, Dak, your parents have been sent to the front line of King Philip's upcoming battle." He slowly shook his head back and forth, even sadder than before. "A place where almost no one survives, I'm afraid."

21

Aristotle's Word

A BOMB had just exploded inside Dak's mind, and he didn't quite know how to deal with it. He heard the greatest and the worst news ever in a single statement from Aristotle. His parents were evidently alive and well, in the same time period as him. And yet they were sent off to a war that would probably kill them.

"Wait . . . um . . . what?" he said, sure he sounded even more ridiculous than he felt.

The great philosopher looked at him with compassion and tenderness, and had him sit back down.

"Listen to me," Aristotle said. "If this is true, then I give you my word that we'll do everything in our power to save them. As surely as we'll save Alexander and his father. Understand?"

Dak nodded. His chest hurt from the stress and worry. But he stayed quiet and waited for the full explanation. Aristotle continued.

"This is a magistrate's report from the office of the hegemon." He held up the scroll and shook it like a flag. "Two people of foreign descent were turned into authorities by a woman and her soldiers. The woman's name is listed as Tilda, and the . . . slaves as the Smyths. Yes, slaves. Now, hear me out."

Dak's eyes had swollen to the size of grapefruits, but he stayed silent.

"Tilda accused them of being runaways and having poisoned their master, a thing I'm most certain that the woman did herself. That's probably how she obtained these soldiers in the first place" — he gave a weary look to the unconscious man on the ground — "by killing their master and . . . *freeing* them to work for her. She's a devious and clever woman."

"But what does that have to do with the front line of some battle?" Sera asked. Dak was too choked up to ask it himself.

"The report has their plea and the resolution," Aristotle answered. "At first they were imprisoned and sentenced to death by poison hemlock — the very fate that befell the great Socrates. In exchange for their lives, they were given duty on the front line of the upcoming war against Persia. Hardly a good trade, but better than outright death, I suppose. Hopefully we can get to them in time. I know King Philip will understand and pull them back. I give you my word, Dak. On Plato's grave, my word."

Dak looked up at the man, his long beard, his salt-and-pepper hair and eyebrows, his wrinkled skin, his wide shoulders, those eyes that said he knew everything worth knowing. Dak understood why Aristotle would go down in history as one of the great thinkers of all the humans who'd ever walked the earth. There was just something . . . majestic about him.

Dak realized something else then, too. It was one thing to be intelligent — to spout facts and figures and generally act like a know-it-all. It was another thing entirely to be wise. And Dak wanted to be more than just smart.

"Dak?" Sera asked. "Are you okay?"

He broke his gaze from the philosopher and turned it toward his best friend. Sera meant everything to him, as much as his parents. Seeing her, still by his side despite everything, and hearing Aristotle's words of wisdom — it all did something to lift his heart. It was going to be okay. Everything. A-okay.

"I'm all right," he finally said, his spirits lifting by the second. "We're close, guys. We're so dang close to wrapping this whole business up. Let's get to King Philip's camp, let's tell him about that Pausanius dude, get my parents back, and warp ourselves back to the nice cozy future we've almost finished creating. Who's in?"

The smile that broke across Sera's face was more full of relief than anything else, but she put her hand out like a quarterback in a football huddle. Dak put his on top of hers.

Riq rolled his eyes and said, "No way. But I'm in."

Dak gave Riq a dramatic glare. "Don't leave us hanging, dude."

With a sigh, Riq laid his hand on top of theirs, and the three friends gave a small cheer.

Aristotle seemed baffled by their hand gesture, but his expression showed a trace of excitement. "Let's find some help for our poor soldier here." The man's breathing was shallow, but steady. "Then we rest, eat, and make preparations. When we're ready, we'll use your magical device to go exactly where we need to go."

∞

Two days later, Sera stood with her friends—and the philosopher, of course—on a rise that stood above a huge sweeping valley that seemed to stretch beyond the horizon. It was like a city with no permanent buildings: Tents filled it from one side to the other. Cookfires, temporary pens for animals, and storage sheds for food and weapons dotted the scene, and men and women streamed through the valley.

"I certainly never thought I'd come to this area," Aristotle said, almost reverently. Sera thought she heard a hint of fear in there somewhere, too. "I've been receiving reports about the hegemon and his growing army for some time now. But to see it firsthand . . . it takes the breath away. I don't like to think about what all those soldiers will do when they march across the continent."

"We're not here to judge," Sera said. She'd struggled plenty with her conscience in the course of fixing the Breaks. She still wondered whether she could have done more for the people she'd met. But the consequences of meddling with history boggled her mind. In the end, all she could do was take the Hystorians at their word, set history on what they claimed was the proper path, and hope for the best.

"No judgment, here," the philosopher replied after a few moments of considering her answer. "I'm just in awe of the power of an army, and I don't like thinking about what happens during the horrors of war and conquest."

"I used to," Dak said quietly. Sera expected him to say more, but he didn't.

Riq turned his back on the sight and faced his companions. "Let's just get the job done. We've come this far and we've done what we were supposed to do. Let's finish it. Nothing could be worse than the Cataclysm."

Aristotle made a harrumphing sound.

"What's our plan of action?" Sera asked her friends. "What do we do first?"

"Oh," Aristotle replied, "I suspect that we don't have to do much of anything."

"What do you mean?" Sera replied.

The man gestured with a nod of the head toward the camp below them. "You'll see soon enough. Our hegemon didn't get to where he is today by letting strangers just appear at his camps without explaining themselves. Thoroughly. Watch and see."

They all turned to face the valley again, and it wasn't more than a minute later that a group of horses came galloping out of the mass of soldiers and up the dry, grassy hill, their hooves kicking up dust in a cloud.

One of the animals broke away from the rest of the crowd and charged in, the man atop its back dressed in light armor, his golden helm hiding most of his face. But the eyes and mouth made Sera think the guy wasn't a very happy person. He looked as if he'd run right over them, but he pulled up his horse at the last second, making it rear back on its two hind legs. Then it settled with a loud neigh and the man spoke in a gruff voice.

"You've crossed onto forbidden ground. Down on your knees. Now!"

Aristotle obviously intended on taking no such treatment. "Listen to me, young man. We are here to speak to the hegemon. My name is—"

"I don't care what your name is, old man!" He pulled out a short whip and slashed it through the air, striking the philosopher across the face. Aristotle yelled out in pain, crumpling to the ground.

"Hey!" Sera screamed. "Do you have any idea who that is?"

The man raised the whip again, and Dak and Riq both jumped in front of her, staring up at the fierce soldier. Sera didn't know if she'd ever seen them do something quite that brave.

The man lowered his arm, but spat, his saliva splashing on all of them. Then he turned to the others who'd come with him. "Tie them up. Gag them. Throw them in the pit. Tomorrow, they hang."

Then he rode off, leaving his minions to do the dirty work.

Gagged and Dragged

EVERYTHING THE jerk of a soldier had said became true, one detail at a time. Dak just hoped that the final order — being hanged — somehow got lost in a loophole. But so far he hadn't seen any nice genius lawyers in fancy suits walking around.

They had an awful, awful couple of hours after the original soldier disappeared back into the army's camp. His men dragged Dak and his friends around and stuffed big wads of cloth in their mouths, making it hard to breathe, much less talk. They tied ropes to their bound wrists, then pulled them along behind their horses. Dak stumbled, fell, got dragged, scrambled to his feet, then stumbled and started the whole process all over again. His friends didn't fare much better. And Aristotle . . .

Seeing what the kind, dignified man went through just about shattered Dak's heart. They gave him no better treatment, no mercy, no respect. He'd yelled his name successfully a couple of times before the soldiers finally gagged him, and all four of them had moaned and groaned and screamed muffled screams since then. But "Aristotle" and "We're friends of Alexander" and "We need to save the king" and "I have to use the bathroom" all came out sounding like *"Mrrrrph rmmm gurgggggrle rrrrmph."*

It was hopeless.

Tears stung Dak's eyes as they dragged him over dry grass, dust and dirt, rocks and pebbles, roots and scattered old bones—which he hoped weren't human. His whole body ached—and his insides felt even worse, watching his friends—by the time they came to a halt at the lip of a giant hole dug into the ground, a roughly rectangular pit in which dozens of people huddled in small groups. Dak saw their terrified eyes, constantly looking up, darting back and forth at the soldiers, probably wondering who'd be the one to finally end their lives.

Dak tried to scream, but it came out as another wimpy muffled moan. He tried to squirm away from the man holding his rope to no avail. He looked at each of his friends—at Sera, at Riq, at Aristotle—hoping that something magical might happen to free them. Desperation and fear boiled in their eyes, as he knew they did in his, too.

The soldiers dragged them to the very edge, then threw them into the pit one by one.

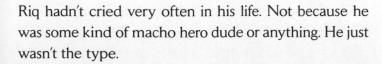

Riq hadn't cried very often in his life. Not because he was some kind of macho hero dude or anything. He just wasn't the type.

But something swelled behind his eyeballs, and it sure felt wet. Eventually, to his own surprise, tears trickled down his cheeks. He would've wiped them away if his hands had been free, but they were bound tightly with rope. So instead he buried his head into his lap as best he could, and cried a little harder.

He didn't completely understand why the sorrow racked him so heavily now, of all times. They'd been through plenty of tough days as they'd traveled throughout history, fixing Break after Break. But these soldiers had seemed so harsh. So brutal. So *mean*. They didn't discriminate their rough treatment—old man, kids, girl, it didn't matter to them. Riq was positive that they treated their animals better, especially the horses.

He was so close, yet so far away from winning his war against the SQ. Stuck in a prison pit, ordered to die in the morning, with no way to tell anyone who they were or why they'd come. And even if they did get out of it, what did it matter? Riq had nowhere to go. Dak and Sera would have to leave him behind. Wasn't he better off dead?

And that was the kicker. That was the truth at the heart of the despair threatening to swallow him up. Sera had been right. He'd preferred the idea of a hero's death to trying to imagine life without family, friends, and the Hystorians' mission.

But he wanted to live. He knew that now. He didn't want to die in this place.

And so, he curled up into a ball as much as possible, and he let himself cry it all out, not caring who saw or heard.

Sera had enough bumps and bruises to last the rest of her life if she had any say in it. But she probably didn't have much say, and she had a feeling that more would be coming.

Aching and wincing, she'd scooted away from where she'd landed after being tossed into the pit, and finally nestled her back against the wall, finding the most comfortable position possible — considering her wrists were tied behind her back. The cloth stuffed inside her mouth was awful, choking her and making it hard to breathe. Several times she'd had to fight the urge to throw up from a gag reflex. She could only imagine how pleasant that would turn out.

Settling her body, she forced herself to relax. Something would work out, she knew it. They still had the Infinity Ring, a miracle in itself. Maybe the soldiers weren't planning on searching them for valuables until they came out of the pit. Or maybe they didn't care, or doubted they had any. Regardless, Sera and her friends had the Ring. And if she could just get her hands free . . .

She struggled a bit but stopped to catch her breath. She took a long look at each of her friends. Riq had curled up into a ball, and she thought his shoulders shook a little. Was he crying? For some reason that hurt worse than the bruises and scrapes. Dak lay on his side, staring at the dirt, breathing slowly and calmly. Aristotle was next to him, sitting up, staring at the edge of the pit as if he expected King Philip or Alexander to appear at any second to rescue them.

She loved these people, her friends, the philosopher . . . She wanted to do whatever it took to get them out, to get them back home. She wanted to win, fix the Prime Break, eliminate the SQ, stop the Cataclysm. She wanted it all so desperately.

And underneath it all, her parents. She could still picture them, as she'd seen them in her Remnants. She knew that whatever power Tilda had over them, they loved her. She just knew it. So if it had been the SQ who had taken her parents from her, then that was all the more reason to keep fighting until the SQ was wiped out of existence.

Dak. Riq. Aristotle. Her parents. Dak's parents. Her uncle. Brint. Mari. The countless others who would be saved if the mission succeeded.

Riq could cry — he deserved to let it all out. Dak could sit and think — he deserved a rest, a break, some time to himself. Aristotle could stare at the sky and hope as much as he wanted.

The rest was up to Sera.

She could do this.

Would do this.

No matter what.

Step by step, piece by piece.

She got to work.

Tedious Work

THE GAG was the first thing to go.

She had to trust her eyes more than ever before in her life. Watching, waiting, watching, looking everywhere—she focused on the soldiers guarding the pit, and forced herself to rely on patience, taking the tiny opportunities when they came. Dak started to sit up when he noticed what she was doing, but she glared at him—they could say more with their eyes and body language than most people could with words—and he went back to lying on the dirty ground.

It took a while—and some serious bending of body parts that she hadn't bent so much since, well, 1850 or so—but she was finally able to reach her hand high enough to grab the wad of cloth in her mouth and pull it out. Choking and coughing, she spun around to face the wall of the pit so that no one could see her. Thirst raked her throat, and it seemed as if the coughs might never stop coming. But they subsided, and she composed herself once again.

She slowly turned around, puffing her cheeks out a bit so that it would look like she still had the gag. A quick survey of the scene up above showed that no guards suspected anything—in fact, they wandered around the pit as if they couldn't care less what anyone below did. But Sera couldn't take any chances.

Riq caught her eye. He'd uncurled from his position and sat staring at her, his face full of questions. That's when Sera made a huge decision. Escaping the pit would be hard enough for one person—impossible for four. Her friends needed to trust that she could find people who knew Aristotle and come back to get them. She hoped they understood. With careful nods of her head and pointing with her eyes, she tried to tell Riq and Dak that she wanted them to create a diversion.

In one corner of the pit, there were enough hand- and footholds in the dug-out dirt that she was certain she could climb up the wall and out. She'd climbed her share of trees throughout the years. Riq and Dak seemed to understand, and started moving to the opposite side of the pit, hands still tied up.

Which reminded Sera of her next task. The ropes binding her wrists didn't seem all that strong. And there were plenty of rocks strewn about the roughly dug prison into which they'd been thrown. She looked around until she found a good one with a sharp edge, then sat over it, head down, like a girl who'd given up on the world and only wanted to cry in pity. Then she started sawing. Back and forth, back and forth, glancing around every few seconds to make sure no soldier had noticed.

A strained, muffled series of sounds came from behind her, and she twisted around to see Aristotle looking directly at her, trying to say something. She shrugged to let him know she couldn't understand, and he stopped making the moaning noise. But then his face took on a calm, commanding presence — almost magical — that seemed to fill the air with some kind of unearthly communication. She felt it, and it encouraged her. He was telling her that he was proud, that he knew she could do this.

She went back to her task, working harder to cut the ropes.

"You there!" a man yelled from the lip of the pit.

Every cell in Sera's body froze solid, and her heart dropped. Still crouching over the rock, she slowly looked up. A soldier stood on the very edge, his toes hanging over. He was pointing, but not at her. He was pointing at Dak and Riq, who bounced on their feet as if they thought they could jump right out of the pit.

"Where do you think you're going?" the guard asked, a hint of cocky amusement in his voice. "Trying to get in some exercise so you'll be nice and fit for the hanging tomorrow?" He bellowed a laugh that made Sera want to strangle him, and some of the other soldiers joined in. One picked up a rock and threw it at Dak, though it missed, kicking up a little puff of dirt where it landed.

Sera couldn't help them, not now. Her best bet was to use the diversion.

She sawed, vigorously, biting her tongue between her lips with the effort. Finally, the rope snapped in two and the frayed fragments fell from her wrists. She quickly squatted over them and kept her hands behind her back, waiting to see if any alarms or shouts arose from the soldiers. But every last one of them continued to mock and throw things at Dak and Riq.

Sera was free. Loose. Too bad she was at the bottom of a huge pit with soldiers all around her.

She moved casually, making sure to avoid quick or jerky movements that might draw attention. Keeping to the lowest, farthest angle of the pit's bottom, she crawled toward the corner, longing for the hand- and footholds like they were a thousand miles away. Dak and Riq had quite a crowd now, causing their diversion without even having to do much. She'd be sure to thank them for all the lumps and bruises they'd have from rocks raining down from above. Thankfully, the guards seemed like they only wanted to taunt them, not hurt or kill them. Most of the ammunition missed by a long shot.

She reached the corner. Freedom awaited ten feet above her. Every soldier she could see had made their way to the other half of the pit, watching the show. She saw Riq notice her, and his eyes said it all before he quickly looked away. He knew she needed something a little more special to ensure no one looked her way.

Riq coiled his legs, then vaulted himself onto Dak, using his shoulders and knees to pummel her best friend. She didn't know if Dak understood what he was doing, but Dak fought back on instinct, and soon they were rolling and tussling comically as the soldiers — and, sadly, the other prisoners — roared with laughter, cheering for one or the other.

Now, Sera thought.

Giving up on any pretense of staying low or being tied with ropes anymore, Sera jumped to her feet and attacked the dirt wall, roughly hewn and filled with places to grab for holds. Some of it crumbled, making her slip several inches at a time, but things stayed solid for the most part. Like a monkey on a jungle gym, she clambered up and reached the top of the pit in no time.

Panting — more from anxiety than the effort of climbing — she didn't waste even a second looking around to see who might've seen her. She spotted a break in a long row of tents nearby, a little alley that led away from the main clearing, where hundreds of people milled about. She headed that direction, sprinting with all the strength left in her body.

She'd made it about halfway when she heard the clamor and yells of the soldiers guarding the pit. Their angry voices rose over the din of the crowd.

They'd spotted her.

2 4

Two Bad Choices

DAK WONDERED if he'd ever have a day again where nothing on his body hurt and there weren't a million things on the planet stressing him out.

Today certainly wasn't it.

He'd already been tired and sore *before* crawling across the dirty floor of the pit with his hands tied. Then you added in the nice element of rocks raining down from the sky, a few of them lucky enough to smack him in the shoulders and back. To top it all off, Riq decided to go insane-wrestler-dude on him, jabbing with his elbows and knees in all kinds of places that didn't feel so hot. Dak had fought back, knowing that it was for Sera — but that didn't mean he had to like it.

And it had worked. He knew it. He'd seen her disappear over the lip of the pit, and she'd had plenty of a head start before the soldiers started yelling and chasing. He knew his friend, and he wouldn't even *allow* the thought of her getting caught to enter his mind. At least he had the pit as a measuring stick — as long as she wasn't hauled back and thrown in, he had to assume she was safe. Unless . . .

Again, he blocked off his mind from terrible possibilities.

Riq lay on his side, facing away from Dak. *The poor guy,* Dak thought. Something about him seemed to suggest he'd finally run out of steam. He reminded Dak of a balloon that held on for as long as it could after a birthday party, clinging to the ceiling, but then eventually sank to the floor, a wilted, crumpled heap of rubber. Dak felt it, too, but he still had hope. Once someone figured out they had Aristotle in their prison pit, surely all would be well in the world again.

The Let's-Throw-Rocks-at-Dak-and-Riq Show had ended as soon as a guard had spotted Sera running away, and most of the guards had left in pursuit. Several returned now, but Dak couldn't tell from their whispers or body language if she'd been captured. The fact that they didn't bring her back, of course, was a very good sign. Unless . . .

One of the soldiers lowered a wooden ladder into the pit, steadied it, then climbed down, followed by two others. Dak shifted around to fully face them, sitting on his rear end, feeling like a lassoed pig. The three guards were armed, and one of them actually had his sword in hand, using only the other as he descended. Though Dak held on to the hope that they had come down for some other purpose, it was quickly dashed. They headed straight for Riq.

Riq noticed them at the last second, jolting and squirming as he tried to get away from them. Useless effort, of course. They snatched him under the arms and hauled him to his feet, then dragged him to the closest wall of the pit, where they—very ungently—threw him back down into the dirt. He landed with a heavy thump and a grunt. Next, they came for Dak, who didn't resist when they did the same thing to him. A few seconds later, he was sitting next to Riq, his backside a little sorer than it had been.

Not surprisingly, Aristotle was their last target, picked up and dragged along to join the two boys with whom he'd arrived at the camp. The soldiers treated him just as roughly, and Dak wanted to hit somebody. Really hard.

Once the three of them were all lined up, the guard who'd come down the ladder brandishing his sword stepped right in front of them. He looked at one of his partners and gave a curt nod. That man came forward and yanked the cloth gags out of each prisoner's mouth. Dak coughed and spat when his came out, feeling the sweet rush of air—which only made him thirstier. The soldier threw the wet, slightly bloody pieces of cloth onto the ground and took a place behind the guy in charge.

"Listen to me well," the man said. "You're the first people to wander into our camps since we heard of . . . ill tidings toward our king and hegemon. On the cusp of the greatest period in Greek history, we have neither the time nor patience to ask who you are or what you want. We've been ordered to take the utmost of precautions, and not to trouble our great leader."

This dude is good at speaking a lot of words without saying *anything,* Dak thought.

"Do you know who I am?" Aristotle asked, his voice a scratchy rasp.

The soldier's face showed no emotion. "I don't care. If you were anyone of importance, you'd know to stay clear of these lands."

"I'm Aristotle!" the philosopher yelled, as loudly as his weakened condition would allow. "I practically raised the son of the great king of whom you speak! I demand you take me to him so we can clear up all this nonsense. I demand you free my friends!"

"Aristotle?" the soldier barked, looking around at his comrades. "Look, men. The greatest philosopher in all the world sprouted wings and flew here from Corinth. His powers are even mightier than I thought."

"I can explain, you fool! The hegemon and his son are in great danger!"

The soldier dropped to one knee and leaned toward them so quickly that Dak recoiled, knocking the back of his head against the hard dirt of the wall.

"I know," the man said. "We know all too well. Which is why we've been ordered to . . . *deal* with lunatics like yourself who come marching into our camp." He stood back up, brushing dust from his knee. "You have two choices, prisoners. And consider yourselves lucky that it's not only one. Circumstances allow for a little leniency, when war is on the morrow."

"What are you talking about?" Dak asked.

The soldier gave him a nasty look, like he didn't care for interruptions. "Your choices are these: death at sunrise, by the gallows, or fight for your redemption on the front line of the king's army when we attack our first foe. We'll need all the bodies we can get up there, and yours will serve justly."

"Either choice is death!" Aristotle yelled.

The soldier shrugged. "People have survived the front line before. Others . . . have not. The choice is yours. Certain death, or death uncertain. Choose."

Dak had his decision before the words even finished coming out of the guy's mouth. His parents. If the magistrate report Aristotle had read to them was true, Dak's parents were on the front line! This was his easiest and best route at reuniting with them. As for how they'd survive the ordeal . . . well, they'd think of something.

"You," the soldier said, pointing at Riq. "Speak. What's your choice?"

"The front line." He answered so quickly that Dak didn't know what to think of it. Riq had been brooding and distant — but Dak had figured you got that way when captured and thrown into a pit. He wished so badly they could just have a few minutes to *talk*.

"A wise choice," the soldier responded, motioning for someone to come and take Riq away. A guard walked over and cut the ropes binding his wrists, then helped him to his feet. "You may take the spear or sword wound that was meant for our real soldiers, or for the hegemon himself. The gods will never forget. Go. Arm him and send him to the front."

"Wait!" Dak yelled. "I'm going with him! That's my choice."

The soldier grunted. "You're barely the size of a rat. But your flesh can capture a spear as well as any other. Fine, take him as well." As the subordinate moved to obey, slashing at the ropes around Dak's wrists, the soldier in charge stepped in front of Aristotle and looked down at him.

"And you, old man? The glorious philosopher who can fly? What say you?"

Aristotle glanced over at Dak with sad, haunted eyes, then at Riq. He answered in a grave, resigned voice.

"I choose death."

2 5

A Very Large Camp

SERA HAD waited a solid hour, hiding in the darkness under a canvas sheet with a bunch of crates and vegetables. It smelled of olives and mildew, and she could barely breathe, but at least it had been a while since she'd heard any sign of pursuit. Maybe she'd done it after all. Escaped the pit and its soldiers. But the hardest part still lay ahead.

Somehow, she had to find the tent of King Philip. She just hoped the man didn't order her killed on the spot once she got there.

Sera poked her head out of the hiding spot and looked around. People walked about everywhere — soldiers, servants, even a few children, doubtless tagging along with parents working on behalf of the army. If she could find some new clothes maybe she could search for the king without drawing too much attention.

Scampering from one hiding place to another, shadow to shadow, she spent the next half an hour or so trying to do just that. She finally hit the jackpot behind a grimy old tent, where a pile of clothing and rags had been thrown out the back, perhaps for washing later. Sera quickly rummaged through it until she found a shirt and pants—ratty, torn, filthy. Luckily, the satchel containing the Infinity Ring was brown and rustic and didn't seem out of place.

And so, the search began.

From tent to tent she went, acting as casual as possible, carrying a box she'd found with a bunch of bandages and ointments—somewhere a medic was wondering where in the world he'd misplaced it. Guards and soldiers were everywhere, but, after all, this was an army camp, so she stopped being alarmed at the sight. The entire camp was a busy beehive—supplies being packed, food being prepared, smiths working on weapons, soldiers practicing with swords and spears, servants hustling about so as not to get trampled.

On Sera went, scouring the place with her eyes to find anything that looked like—

And then she spotted it.

One tent towered over the others around it, but she hadn't been able to see it before because of so many smaller tents obscuring her view. The one she saw now was grand and painted in many colors and had a row of soldiers guarding all four sides of it. If there'd ever been a tent fit for a king, that was it.

She made her way toward it, racking her brain for an idea of how to actually get inside. All she needed was five minutes—no, maybe even *one* minute—with

King Philip before she could convince him. She knew it. Especially if Alexander had already arrived — he'd remember her for sure. And know that she was a friend to his mentor.

Getting more scared with each and every step she took toward the front flaps of the huge tent, she didn't allow herself to slow. Somehow, someway, she would get inside. Sometimes, being a young person had its advantages — no one would take her as a real threat.

She was about thirty feet away, squeezing past a compact crowd of people going about their business, when a commotion to the far right of the tent caught her attention. Several soldiers were shouting and pushing their way toward the very spot to which Sera was headed. When they finally broke free and came into her line of view, she stopped and sucked in a quick take of air.

It was Alexander, dragging a soldier — the man who'd captured Sera and her friends — by the scruff of his shirt. As for Alex, he looked as angry as he had when he'd left them back at the palace of his mother, charging away on his horse, Bucephalus. Several other soldiers were with him, and bringing up the rear was Aristotle, completely free of bindings.

What in the world . . . ? She had no idea what to think of it, especially upon seeing that Dak and Riq weren't with him. That scared her to no end.

Alexander dragged the soldier all the way to the front of the king's tent and then threw him onto the ground.

"Any man who can't tell the greatness of Aristotle on sight doesn't deserve to live!" he yelled, then reared back like he was going to kick the poor guy, but stopped at the last second, looking back at his master, who was shaking his head back and forth. "Mercy, then. Get back to your duties, soldier."

The man, though obviously hurt, was more than happy to oblige. He jumped to his feet and disappeared quickly into the crowd. Sera acted on instinct, knowing that her chance lay before her like a gift from the Greek gods. She ran forward, straight toward the heir to the king.

"Alexander!" she yelled. "Aristotle! It's me, Sera!"

A couple of guards around Alex jolted to attention — one of them lifted a spear as if to chuck it right at Sera. But Alexander quickly reached out and stopped him.

"No," he ordered. "I know this girl. She's a friend."

And just like that, Sera was officially free. Not able to help herself, she ran to Aristotle and threw her arms around him, hugging the man as if he were the uncle she missed so much from back home. He returned the hug, soothing her with soft words.

"What happened?" she asked, pulling back a bit. "Where are Dak and Riq?"

A grave look shadowed the philosopher's face. "It's been a very complicated few hours. I . . . volunteered myself to die — as silly as it sounds — because I hoped I'd be brought before the king or one of his council members as a matter of policy. Someone finally — *finally* —

recognized me and informed Alex, who arrived just yesterday. However . . . as for your friends . . ."

"What?" Sera yelled, her heart forgetting how to beat.

"It was too late when I had them sent for. They've been taken to the front line, and communication on that front is poor to say the least. But don't worry, I'll be sure to get them back—as well as the boy's parents—before any real fighting takes place. Please try not to worry."

He must've read her face, because the worry almost engulfed her. Not to mention the guilt. If she hadn't escaped from the pit, she could've used the Infinity Ring to whisk them all away once they were sent to the front line.

But then she remembered the reason they were here to begin with.

"Have you told him everything?" she asked Aristotle, throwing a wary glance toward Alexander.

The philosopher shook his head slightly. "He knows enough, but the boy seems to have a hard time believing I'm not a cracked pot."

"I'm standing right here, you know," Alexander replied. "Listen, both of you. I have more guards around me than I'd ever need. I am keeping an eye on my father. All is well. Let's go inside and plan our strategies. War is coming."

Aristotle gave Sera a look that was almost comical, a What're-you-gonna-do look. They followed Alexander and the rest of the soldiers and guards into the grand tent of King Philip. Upon entering, Sera's chest swelled with awe. There were fancy carpets and bronze bowls with red-hot coals and thick pillows strewn about for sitting. And, most majestic of all, was the king himself — it had to be him — sitting in a gilded chair, gazing intently at a map rolled open on his lap. Sera was excited to meet him and wished Dak could be there with her — but as it turned out, there was no time for introductions.

The king stood when he saw Alexander, and gruffly handed the map over to a young page waiting beside him.

"Son!" he yelled, with not a hint of joy at seeing him. "Your timing is impeccable. I've just been told that the Persians have taken the initiative and are moving in rapidly. Our front line will soon be under attack."

26

The Sound of War

DAK HAD tried to hold on to hope as he, Riq, and a large group of others were sent in a horse-drawn cart through the massive army toward the front line. He kept telling himself that Sera would make a difference, figure out what to do, save them. That he and Riq would find his parents and have a happy reunion, then hang out until someone figured out that this group of people from the future didn't belong on any side of an army, let alone the front.

But that hope was fleeting. As Dak saw the countless soldiers and weapons and horses, and the bleak looks on the faces of those ready to fight, fear filled him. He realized through and through just how mighty the army was — which meant whomever they were prepping to fight must be scary as heck, too. What could Sera possibly do to save them from this mess?

They jostled along, weaving their way through a small break in the sea of soldiers, heading toward their deaths. Dak just hoped that he could be with his parents when it happened. That they could die together.

"You're looking awfully glum," Riq said.

"I should be more happy, huh? I mean, check this out. I'm about to get killed in a famous historical war. Yippee, right?"

"Right."

Dak stared at the linguist, a guy who'd sneakily become one of his best friends. He seemed to have so much going on behind his eyes that curiosity won out over all that I'm-about-to-die stuff.

"What in Rasputin's name are you thinking about over there?" he asked.

Riq yawned, then slightly shook his head. "Just wondering what I can do for this world."

Dak didn't know what answer he'd expected, but certainly not *that*. "What you can do for the world? Really? I'd say you've done quite a bit so far. And, hey, if we die, there's still a pretty decent chance that Alexander doesn't—especially with Sera on the loose. So, we *saved* the world, dude. If I had some root beer, we'd celebrate." He was trying to cheer things up, and he was afraid he was doing a poor job of it.

"No, man, you don't get it." Riq stared off into the distance as he spoke. "Yeah, I think you're right that we'll fix the Prime Break. Avoid the Cataclysm and all that. But that doesn't mean that the world still doesn't have a lot of room for improvement."

Dak nodded slowly, showing his best face of contemplation. "Well said. If somehow we don't get gored by a hundred spears, we can start a charity."

Riq laughed—the worst courtesy laugh Dak had ever heard. "Yeah. But I just wonder about this time and place. About King Philip and Alexander. It seems like . . . I don't know. It seems like they need better guidance. With all this power, they could do a lot of good for civilization. For the future."

"What're you trying to say?" Dak asked. Something in Riq's tone had scared him.

Riq never got a chance to answer.

People up ahead had started shouting, all their voices scrambling together to make it impossible for the translator in Dak's ear to pick up anything. A tension seemed to pass through the crowds of soldiers like a visible wave. And somewhere, rising in volume, was the sound of thunder. A rolling, thumping noise that shook the ground.

The guard in charge of the horses that'd been leading their cart turned around to face them, his face snapped tight with fear, eyes wide.

"They're attacking us!" he screamed, then lifted his sword and, for some reason, severed the ropes connecting the horses to the cart. He slapped their rears and shooed them back in the direction from which they'd just come. "Get out!" he shouted at Dak and everyone else. "Grab your weapons and get out! There's no more time! By authority of the hegemon, I order you to make your way to the front line and help us stop the enemy's charge. *NOW!*"

The soldier held his sword out as if he'd chop off the head of the first person who refused to obey. Riq was already on his feet, reaching out to help Dak stand. They grabbed their own swords—rusty and dented and dull—from a pile in the front of the cart. Then they jumped to the ground to join the others—most of them too old, too young, or too frail to fight off a chicken, much less an army of Persians.

Terror rattled Dak's heart, made it hard to breathe. But somehow Riq was keeping his cool, like he'd done this a thousand times.

"Come on," he said to Dak. "Come on, we can survive this. Stay by me, and we can do it. Come on."

As they started running through the melee, going in the direction ordered by the guard, Dak struggled for every breath. He knew Riq was lying, saying whatever it took to make him feel better. And Dak loved him for it.

They ran off to war.

∞

Sera had stood to the side of the cavernous tent for twenty minutes or so, watching the king, his son, Aristotle, and many others excitedly talk about what was going on just a few miles from where they stood. They'd been planning to take the fight wherever they needed to go—and soon—but their enemies had brought it to them instead. The hegemon seemed just fine with that, judging by the expression of something like glee on his face as he pointed at maps and barked orders left and right. The only times he ever paused were to take big gulps of wine from a pewter cup—which his page continually refilled.

A soldier came through the front flap of the tent and didn't wait for permission to speak before he yelled what he had come to say. "They've broken through the front line! It's all-out war!"

Sera's heart shriveled like a rotted raisin. Dak. Riq. Dak's parents. How could they possibly survive? Her only hope was that maybe they hadn't gotten far before the fighting had begun. Maybe they were stuck in the middle of the huge army safe for the moment.

Dak, she thought. *Oh, Dak. Riq. Please be safe. Please!* She didn't know what she'd do if she lost her best friends after all they'd been through.

The hustle and bustle of planning and shouting orders continued inside the tent. Every minute or so, a soldier would leave, sprinting, ready to carry those orders out into the field. At the same rate, others would return with progress reports. The whole thing seemed like chaos, but Sera was sadly familiar with it by now. It seemed to her that war was all too similar across cultures and epochs.

She then noticed something. Something very odd, that everyone else—amid that very chaos—had failed to realize yet. The king had sat down. Just a few minutes earlier, he'd been animated, throwing around his arms, stomping his feet, yelling and screaming. Now he sat as others continued in his place. And he looked weak. Pale. He slumped in the gilded chair, seeming to shrink right before her eyes. Every ounce of blood had drained from his face.

And then she knew.

Poison.

The wine.

Then, to her horror, she saw Alexander with a cup in his hand. The page must've just handed it to him—his hands had been empty before. But now he had some of the wine. He was raising it to his lips.

"No!" she screamed. She was running. Jumping over bunched-up carpets. Pushing people out of her way. The cup was almost to Alexander's lips. She ran harder, the tent suddenly feeling like it was a mile wide. "No!" she screamed again.

Alexander opened his mouth.

Sera took another step.

Alexander tilted the cup, tilted his head.

Sera reached him.

Diving, she lashed her hand out and knocked the cup away from the man's hand, sending a spray of red wine all over the place. The cup fell to the ground with a thump and a bounce, and wine fell like droplets of rain onto the carpet. Sera landed and rolled, now on her back, looking up at Alexander, who glared down at her with more surprise than fury.

"What in the name of Zeus?" he called out.

But all she could do was smile. Despite it all, despite knowing her friends might be dead, despite the loss of the king, she smiled—a thing of triumph, not glee.

In that moment, without a shred of doubt, Sera knew she had just prevented the Cataclysm. Once and for all. Mission complete.

27

The Rage of War

DAK HAD once daydreamed of moments like this—so often. Lying in bed, sitting in class, staring at a book without comprehending the words. Imagining himself in one of history's great wars, wielding a sword, bearing down on his enemies with all the wrath of a Greek god on the cusp of defeat.

If he'd learned one thing during his travels, it's that real war was far from glamorous. This battle was no exception. Most of the time, he just tried to avoid getting trampled by people on his own team. And he'd yet to stab or maim so much as a big toe. Sticking close to Riq, they weaved their way through the chaos of battle, doing their very best not to kill *or* be killed.

An enemy soldier loomed over them, appearing out of a thick knot of clashing warriors, a spear raised with both hands. His face wore a scowl of hatred, like he'd been oppressed his whole life by two kids from the future. Riq swung his sword upward just as the man's thrust came down, shattering the wood of the weapon into a dozen pieces. The man screamed bloody murder, but a tide of battling bodies swept him away, and Riq and Dak ran, threading through and dodging the clashes as best they could. Dak had no idea where Riq was trying to go, but he had a sudden and desperate dependency on the older boy.

Dust filled the air, along with screams and grunts, the clang of metal against metal, the peal of horses in pain, and thunderous roars of battle that all melded together into a chorus of war and rage. As much as Dak loved history and reading about wars, he'd never again wish to be in the middle of one.

Soldiers attacked them. Dak and Riq survived moment to moment, deflecting weapons, dodging, running. On they went.

They broke into a rare clearing, and what Dak saw before him made the entire world freeze into a bubble of silence and wonder, every sound a buzz in his ears, barely heard over the hammering of his heart.

Ten feet away, his parents lay on the ground, clasped in each other's arms.

∞

Sera rode on the back of a horse, her arms holding on to Aristotle's waist. She gripped him so hard that her muscles ached, but she was terrified of falling off the charging beast. Alexander rode beside them on Bucephalus, the new king standing in the stirrups, his right arm brandishing a sword forward as if it had the power to cut through the sea of battling soldiers before them, which seemed to stretch to every horizon. Other soldiers, also on horses, flanked them on both sides as they surged ahead, moving like an icebreaker ship hacking its way through the Arctic.

Sera just squeezed her grip and rested her head on Aristotle's back, wanting to close her eyes — as if that would make it all go away. The scenes of battle — the horror of it — made her wince. It was all just so awful. She hoped — desperately — that they could achieve what Alexander had promised once her explanations had been given in the tent: to find Dak and Riq, to find Dak's parents, and to take them away from the raging war. To take them to safety.

Sera had saved Alexander's life, though not until she'd seen the hegemon die from the poison. But perhaps that's what was fated to happen all along. For *Alexander* to lead the armies of Greece, here and now. For Alexander the Third to become Alexander the . . . Great.

"There!" Aristotle roared, shockingly loud considering the noise around them. "I see them!" He was pointing madly to their right. And then came the words that eased the cinch around her heart for the first time in hours. "They're still alive!"

Alexander altered course.

∞

Dak hadn't lived that many years when it really got down to it. But in his decade or so of life — especially since being recruited to the Hystorians — he'd experienced a lot of different emotions. Happy and sad. Victorious and disappointed. Despair. Anger. Love. Hate. Lots of stuff.

But never, not once, had he ever felt the thing that swelled within him at the sight of his parents, alive, huddling in each other's arms as armies fought around them. It was a thing that he'd never be able to explain and would probably never feel again. Tears stung his eyes and a wonderful pain filled his chest. There they were.

His parents.

"Mom!" he yelled. "Dad!" He was already sprinting toward them, almost oblivious to the danger that swarmed in from all directions. From what he could see, it looked as if his mom had tripped and fallen over a wounded soldier, and then his dad had joined her, practically on top of her, like a shield.

Dak slid to the ground on his knees, coming to a stop just a few inches short of his parents. Finally, they both turned their heads to see their son. Even as they did so, two men clashed swords right above them, the crack of metal against metal vibrating through the air. Luckily, the soldiers, swords locked, moved to the side. The sounds of war everywhere else raged on.

"Dak," his dad said. The poor man's face was pale with worry, his skin tight, fear burning in his eyes. The word came out almost as a whisper, more disbelief than anything else.

"You're safe now," Dak replied, having no clue what else to say.

His mom saw him, but her whole face was pinched up and tears streamed from her eyes. Finally, Dak just lunged forward, and they all hugged, gripping one another and crying and trying to say words but none that came out intelligible. Death and mayhem surrounded them, but for that moment, they were all alive, and they were together. After months of chasing through time after time.

They were together.

∞

It took a universe of effort for Riq to stand still and allow Dak to have his moment with his parents. He couldn't think of a much worse place to have a family reunion, but the Smyths hadn't had much choice in the matter. Finally, when the hug and joy had gone on for a good twenty seconds, Riq had to speak up.

"Dak!" he called out. "None of this will do much good if we get ourselves killed. We need to protect ourselves!" He did a quick turn, his weapon held out, ready to fight off anyone close. They'd been lucky enough to find themselves in a random clearing of the fight, but that wouldn't last much longer.

Dak scrambled to his feet, slyly wiping a tear on his shoulder. He helped his parents stand up, then they all moved closer to Riq, forming a circle with their backs to one another. A man with a veil over his face, spear held high, charged at them, screaming words too laced with bloodlust to comprehend. Fear thumped inside Riq, but he kept it at bay, waiting, forcing himself to remain still until the very last second.

With a yell, he lifted his sword with both hands, striking the spear just before it slammed into his own chest. The man was taken off guard, losing his balance as he tried to rebound from his spear being swatted upward, and he fell flat on his back. Riq raised his sword and screamed, glowering with all the anger he could muster at an enemy he didn't know. It was just enough that the guy rolled away, got up, and ran back into the thicker melee of battling soldiers.

"Not bad," Mr. Smyth said. "Looks like you guys have picked up a few tricks while chasing us through time."

"Lovely spot for a family vacation," his wife added.

Riq didn't have time to respond. The man he thought he'd just defeated reappeared, and this time he had seven or eight of his companions with him. After pushing his way through a wall of clashing soldiers, the guy raised his spear and pointed its sharp tip right at Riq.

And then they all charged in.

28

Upon the Horses

SERA'S ELATION at hearing that her friends were still alive only lasted a moment. When she finally got a good look at them — when Alexander changed their course and the other horses followed — she saw that Dak and the others were backed together in a group and a crowd of robed soldiers was coming at them with weapons raised.

"Dak!" she screamed, as if that could help him at all. "Riq! Run!" She felt so hopeless, and the words sounded stupid. Trying to will the horses to gallop faster, she stared, her heart rattling with terror.

The leading man — holding a spear out in front of him as if he wanted to pole vault — reached Dak's group first, but Riq took a step forward, swinging an old, dented sword in an arc that snapped the spear into two pieces. Sera cheered loudly before she could help herself, and despite knowing that it'd been a lucky shot and that plenty of death was coming in right behind the first guy. Swords were raised. Battle yells were roared. For a split second, Sera caught a glimpse of Dak's face, and it was painted white with fear. She felt such a rush of concern and love for her friend that it felt like she might explode.

And then Alexander was on them.

His mighty horse, Bucephalus, charged into the crowd of onrushing soldiers, tossing them to the sides like stalks of corn. They scrambled and dove, and a couple of them weren't lucky enough to avoid the hammering hooves of the beast. Riq turned away from it, and shoved Dak and the Smyths to safety, even as Alexander stood up in his stirrups and started swinging away with his sword, cutting down the enemy at a speed that seemed impossible. His companions joined in, just as more of the robed fighters appeared to help their friends. In a matter of seconds, it had turned into an all-out battle of clanging swords and shouts of pain.

"Go get them!" Sera yelled into Aristotle's ear. "Get them!" She knew he understood, and their horse leapt toward Dak and the others even before the words had finished coming out of her mouth.

∞

Dak had a million thoughts go through his mind in an instant. Mostly he was fixated on how ridiculously brave Riq had become, fighting off dudes with that old sword of his. For a long moment, it felt as if Riq was all that stood between them and certain death.

But then there were horses. Alexander. Chaos. Swords swinging and men screaming.

Then he heard his name.

"Dak!"

He looked up and saw a horse coming right at him, leaping over fallen soldiers. Aristotle had the reins, a fierceness gripping his features. Sera was behind him, holding on to him with one arm and pointing at Dak with the other.

"Mom, Dad, quick!" he yelled at his parents. He grabbed them by the arms and pulled them close, then waited for Aristotle's horse to pull up right beside them. "Quick, get on!"

They tried to complain, tried to insist he get on first, but he ignored them, finding strength he never knew he had, practically lifting them onto the horse himself. Sera had slipped off, helping out.

"What are you doing?" he yelled at her, even as his mom was able to finally get her legs situated correctly on both sides of the horse.

"You can't fit that many people!" she answered, with a quick jerk of her head behind them. Another couple of horses were waiting for them, their riders keeping all enemy soldiers at bay with their swords. Dak made sure his parents were secure behind Aristotle, then swatted the horse's rear end to get it going. With a loud whinny it galloped off, dodging soldiers as it went. Dak followed Sera toward another horse and rider that had come with the philosopher.

Dak noticed that Riq had not backed down from the fight. He stood shoulder to shoulder with Alexander and his companions.

"Riq!" he yelled at him. "We need to go! Come on!"

His friend swatted away a sword, then turned to look

back. "No! Just go! I'll make sure you can escape!" But he'd hardly said the last word before he vaulted into the air, lifted by a man on a white horse that had come out of nowhere, breaking through the line of defense set up by Alexander and his partners.

"Riq!" Dak shouted, this time with horror. An enemy soldier had just single-handedly picked Riq up like a bag of leaves and thrown him across the saddle of the horse. The man kicked the sides of the animal and it burst into a gallop, charging away.

Dak knew they had to follow, but he had barely looked up at the horse he'd hoped to ride with Sera when a thrown spear hurtled through the air and landed with a sickening *thunk* in the friendly rider's chest. He groaned, his eyes rolling up into his head, then he toppled off the horse and onto the ground. It was like the entire world had just shifted on its plates. Dak held off the panic that tried to paralyze him. He had to act — Alexander and everyone else were too busy fighting.

"Come on, Sera!" he yelled, motioning for her to jump onto the now riderless animal.

She didn't argue or hesitate — throwing a foot into the stirrup, she was up there in three seconds. Dak followed, almost knocking her off when he swung his leg around to the other side. He'd planned on being in front, but somehow she'd ended up in the driver's seat.

"Ride!" he yelled.

Sera turned to him and shouted back, "What about your parents?"

"They'll be safe with Aristotle!"

"And Alexander?"

Dak shook with impatience. "Look at the dude — he's in his element. Now ride!"

"You got it." Sera shook the reins and made a nickering sound that somehow rose above the din of battle around them, and the horse leapt into motion, jumping over wounded soldiers as it fell into pursuit, chasing after Riq.

Dak held on tight.

29

A Sea of War

As much as Alexander was in his element, Sera was far out of hers, and she knew it. Holding on to the reins so fiercely that her fingers hurt, she kept her eyes riveted to what lay before her, directing as best she could: swinging around one-on-one clashes, hearing the ring of sword against sword, jumping over fallen soldiers, dashing through every break that opened up. All the while, following the man who'd taken Riq.

Luckily, the horse they rode seemed battle tested and intelligent, knowing what to do and acting even before Sera tried to "drive" the reins. Most people in the army were too busy attacking or defending to pay them notice, and on they rode. Dak was hurting her middle, he squeezed so tight from behind, but it was comforting to know he was there and safe. For now, at least.

A soldier was running toward the path right ahead of them, coming in at an angle so he could intercept them. Dak yelled for her to look out.

"I see him!" she called back. "Put your foot to good use!"

She felt Dak shift behind her, leaning toward the right a bit. She leaned the other direction to maintain their balance. She didn't know why this one particular soldier had singled them out. Maybe he just wanted some easy prey. But he came up to their side just as she rode the horse through a narrow clearing between major clashes of fighting soldiers. With a scowl that chilled her blood, he pulled out a dagger and made as if to throw it, aiming.

"Now!" Sera yelled.

Dak kicked out and knocked the knife away, then shifted his foot the other direction to smack the guy in the face so he couldn't attempt to pull them off. Screaming obscenities, the man fell into a patch of mud just in time for two soldiers to trip and fall on top of him. Sera caught only a brief glance, but no one in the trio seemed too happy about the situation.

Dak had almost slipped completely off, but he righted himself behind her. She could feel the heavy breaths in his chest as he leaned into her and got his grip again.

They'd gained ground on Riq despite the little altercation. Sera willed the horse to go even faster.

∞

Surprisingly, Riq felt no fear. Maybe, after overcoming so much, he'd finally grown cold to terror. Hardened up, grown thicker skin. Whatever the reason, he felt a calming wave slow his pulse as he was jostled along, thrown across the back of the enemy's horse like a big bag of grain. The man who'd heaved him off the ground was shockingly strong, having quashed every tiny effort Riq had made to squirm out of the position. When it proved impossible, he'd decided to wait it out—wait until the perfect opportunity presented itself.

He didn't understand why he'd been taken. Maybe this guy had seen a chance to have a prisoner—maybe he thought Riq was a close friend to Alexander since they'd been fighting side by side. Maybe the dude just wanted an excuse to get away from the battle and save his own skin.

It didn't matter. Riq had no intention of reaching whatever the soldier's destination happened to be. Risking the man's wrath, he turned his head to look back in the direction from which they'd come. The horse jumped over something just as he did it, and his chin banged against the leather of the saddle. He bit his lip and cried out in pain. The rider punched him, right in the kidneys. The pain was intense—a flash of agony.

But then Riq saw Sera. And Dak behind her. Sitting on a horse. Coming at him. Coming *for* him.

My friends, he thought.

∞

"Almost there!" Dak yelled, every muscle in his body tense. There was something amazing about riding on a horse like this—especially through a sea of fighting armies. The adrenaline pumping through him seemed like it had been amped up a million times over.

"What do we do?" Sera shouted without turning back to him. Dak knew keeping the horse under control had to take a ridiculous amount of concentration.

Dak had no idea how to answer. "Just get close! Something brilliant will pop into my head!"

She muttered something that he couldn't hear. He imagined it was something to the effect of "We'd be better off using *my* head." But this was Dak's moment. He felt as if the others had saved him so often and had, whether meaning to or not, always treated him like the annoying little brother. But today he planned on becoming the big brother.

The sounds of war — screams and clanks and yells and grunts — filled the air as they rushed past countless soldiers battling one another. Sometimes the sight of it was gruesome, and Dak had no idea who was winning. But they kept their course, dodging and weaving and jumping whenever they needed to. Riq was only a few feet ahead of them now, the dirt kicked up by that horse's hooves dusting the nose of their own horse. The thunderous roar of their galloping thumped in Dak's ears.

Then, just like that, he knew what he was going to do. And he was glad he didn't have time to think it over.

"Pull to the left!" he yelled at Sera. "Get as close as you can!"

Thankfully, she didn't ask for any more details and guided the horse accordingly. Seeing her trusting him like this, following his command, made the whole ordeal worth it. Unless he died. He really didn't want to die.

The horse kicked into high gear and lunged ahead, pulling even with Riq and his captor, who looked over at them like he'd just seen an alien spaceship zoom in. He yelled something unintelligible, then reached for the sword that hung from his waist, holding Riq down with his other hand. But Dak wasn't going to let him get his weapon or do anything else.

Holding on to Sera's shoulders for leverage, he brought both of his legs up until he could get his feet under him, then crouched on the saddle. The soldier had grabbed the hilt of the sword, had started to pull the weapon from its sheath. Dak straightened his legs with full force and jumped, leaping across the narrow gap between the horses and slamming headfirst into the shoulder of Riq's captor. The man slipped several inches but then grabbed the pommel of his saddle, fighting for balance. Dak wrapped his arms around him and fought like crazy, tugging at the big guy with what little strength he had, trying to get him off the horse.

Riq was free now, but in too awkward of a position to do much. Dak could see him attempting to get into a sitting position, but the horse's jouncing movement slammed him back onto his stomach. Dak kept struggling, avoiding the man's punches and elbows, weaving and ducking his head in all directions. Squeezing as tightly as possible with his arms lassoed around the soldier's chest, Dak picked up his flailing feet and settled their soles against the side of the horse. Then he jerked backward with his arms and kicked out with his feet.

It worked.

He and the soldier tumbled off of the horse and slammed into the ground.

∞

Riq scrambled, twisting this way and that until he could finally get in a position to throw himself into the seat of the now-empty saddle. Filled with dread at what might've happened or would happen to Dak, he grabbed the reins and pulled back, too much too fast. The horse reared up on its back legs, kicking its front ones, and Riq toppled off as well, landing with a graceless thump onto the ground.

But then he was on his feet. Running. He saw Dak and the soldier who'd kidnapped him each struggling to gain the upper hand. Even as he looked, Riq saw the man climb on top, pinning Dak down with his legs.

"No!" Riq shouted, running harder.

The soldier pulled a dagger out of some hidden pocket, lifted it toward the sky, ready to drive it down and end Dak's life. Riq was too far away. His throat almost ripped from the scream that burst out of his lungs. The man's arms swung with a mighty force toward Dak's chest.

There was a blur of movement, a flash of brown, an inhuman squeal of rage.

Like magic, from nowhere, Sera and her horse jumped out of the nearby fray, leaping through the air. The animal's front hooves crashed into the soldier on top of Dak, throwing him violently off and sending the dagger in a flying spin until it landed with a thud in a patch of flattened grass. The soldier lay still to the side of Dak, dazed or dead, Riq didn't care.

He picked up his friend, finding strength from somewhere deep, and threw him onto the horse behind Sera. Then he himself used a stirrup to join them, leaping onto the horse's back, reaching forward to squeeze both Sera and Dak in one big hug.

"Go!" he yelled, and they went.

30

The King's Right-Hand Man

DAK REALIZED now that he knew almost nothing about war and its horrors. But there was one thing he'd come to understand, and it was hard-won wisdom: Rarely were there true winners in a battle — what with the lives lost, injuries sustained, and loved ones devastated. But he had a feeling that the armies of Alexander would cross the world and do good things in the long run, despite the losses and heartache. And, at least for one day, they'd taken a successful step and driven back the armies of Persia and their surprise invasion.

Now he sat with his friends around a fire, its smoke floating up like a stream of ghosts to disappear out of a hole in the top of King Philip's tent. The former hegemon, now dead. Alexander was king now, and he sat on a stool, staring at the flames, probably brooding about how much his life had changed in such a short time. He'd never wept for his father, but his face had shown it all, especially when he'd ridden back into camp atop his majestic horse, Bucephalus.

As for Dak and his friends, they'd ridden fast and hard, finally finding a break in the battle — enough to get outside the main sea of soldiers and take the long way back to camp, where they'd finally been treated with the respect and care they deserved. Dak was exhausted, sapped of energy, and aching from a million cuts and bruises. Riq and Sera were no better by the looks of it. They'd hardly said a word since returning.

But they'd won. As far as they could tell, they'd won.

The Great Breaks had all been fixed.

Dak was nervous about going back to the future. A small part of him dreaded it, worried that they'd pop into a nightmare of a world, on the brink of collapse and destruction. But most of him — all the good parts — knew they'd succeeded. How he could be so sure, he had no clue. But, deep down, he just knew it.

Aristotle looked the worst out of all of them. The man stood up, his robes and hair filthy, his face marked with a dozen small wounds.

"We must return to Corinth," he said. "Olympias and Pausanius have been taken there, ready to be judged for their crimes against our former king. We have a long journey ourselves." He raised a hand to stop Sera before she could even get the words out. "No, my child. My days using the Infinity Ring are over, I'm afraid. We'll be traveling the old-fashioned way."

Dak liked the sound of that. He liked it a lot. A trip through Greece? Seeing the sights? His spirits lifted a thousand times. Plus, what was the rush getting back to their own day? They had all the time in the world. He snickered at his brilliant thought, something he'd been waiting a long time to think.

"What do you think about your parents disappearing?" Alexander suddenly asked — the man rarely spoke, and when he did, he made you want to jump through hoops to give him a good answer. "Troubling, is it not?"

Actually, it wasn't. Sera had warned him that it would happen, which had given him an opportunity to say good-bye to his mom and dad before they'd ghosted out. Because they had been cut loose in the time stream without the Ring, it was the Great Breaks that had kept them stuck in the past, warping from one Break to another until only the Prime Break remained. And with that now fixed, the fabric of reality was able to heal itself. That meant anomalies like Dak's parents were being sent back where they belonged.

At least, that's what Sera had said. Dak was too tired to doubt any of it.

"I'm not worried," he told Alexander, not wanting to start a discussion about the intricacies of time travel. "My mom and dad have always had their own way of doing things. We'll . . . see them soon enough."

The new king nodded, surely thinking about how he'd just lost his own parents. But he was too focused on the huge task ahead of him to let anything daunt him for long. "I admire your spirit, boy. I liked you from the instant I saw you climb the statue of Plato. May the gods bless you all." He stood up as if to leave — even though it was his own tent now — but Riq didn't let him go.

"Wait," he said. "Alex — I mean, King . . . Lord hegemon . . ." He looked at Dak in desperation, not knowing how to address him.

"Just call him Alexander," Dak replied, loving every second of it.

"Speak your mind," the king ordered. "I'm weary and need to rest for the battles to come."

Riq straightened, his chest puffing out. "I'd like to join your army. Fight by your side."

Dak and Sera were on him in an instant, throwing out questions left and right. The world suddenly felt surreal and unstable again, as if the Breaks hadn't been corrected after all. What could he possibly be talking about?

"You guys, stop," Riq said quietly. But something in his face silenced Dak completely, and he knew there'd be no changing his friend's mind. Riq wasn't going back with them. "Both of you knew this was coming. My future was altered, and I can't go back." He lowered his voice. "But I can have a future here, and I can make a difference. These people need my help. I think their intentions are good, but they obviously have a lot to learn about civility and treating other cultures with respect. I can do them a lot of good."

"But . . ." Dak started, and didn't finish. His heart hurt. Sera's face had melted into the saddest frown he'd ever seen. "But," he repeated.

"Trust me, okay?" Riq replied, reaching out to squeeze both Dak's and Sera's shoulders. "This is what I have to do."

"What about Kisa?" Sera asked. "You could go and be with her and the Maya."

Riq shook his head. "No. She has her own destiny. Mine is here. To help Alexander change the world. And hey, what's the big deal? You have a time-travel device. You can come visit me anytime you want. Duh." He smiled, then turned his gaze to the king. "Will you have me, hegemon?"

Alexander, tired and worn out as he might be, looked every bit a king as he walked over and stood in front of Riq. "I'd be honored to have you by my side. I really would. And there you'll be, always, to the four corners of the earth. But I'm giving you a new name, a . . . *Greek* name. You are a builder, a maker, and so I name you after Hephaestus, god of fire. From this day forward you'll be known as Hephaestion. Be back here at dawn to plan our next move." And with that, Alexander left, leaving his own tent to Riq and the others for their good-byes.

Dak felt no shame as he hugged his two best friends in the world and bawled his eyes out.

Dinosaurs

SERA LOOKED up, way up, and saw something that she surely never imagined she would: the long, long neck of an Apatosaurus. Its gigantic mouth munched and munched as it tore the leaves off of a tree.

She wasn't dreaming. This was real. And it had all been Aristotle's idea.

"Cool," Dak whispered, staring above with his mouth hanging open like the cargo door of a giant airplane. "Cool."

Olympias — mother of Alexander the Third, wearer of amethysts, plotter of murders — sat upon a stone, her hands and feet bound by a material that the great philosopher said would dissolve within a few hours. Right next to her, Pausanius himself sat, tied up and brooding like a punished child. He was an ugly guy, and Sera was anxious to warp back to the time of Greece so she wouldn't have see his traitorous face anymore.

"How could you do this to us?" Olympias asked, as calm, cool, and collected as Sera had ever seen her.

"How will you go throughout the rest of your lives, living with the guilt of leaving us here to be eaten by these monsters?"

"Oh, stop your complaining," Dak answered, finally pulling his gaze from the enormous beast that towered above them. "This region is dominated by herbivores, and there's plenty of food and fresh water for you guys to live long happy years together. You deserve each other. Just be glad that Aristotle didn't let them throw you in the dark dungeons, like the hegemon ordered. This is paradise."

Sera did feel a *little* guilty, but Dak made a great point. Alexander had felt so utterly betrayed by his own mother that he'd wanted the harshest of punishments. Olympias and Pausanius were actually getting off easy. Way easy. Most civilizations would've put them to death. In fact, Alexander intended to tell everyone that Pausanius, at least, had been killed. The new hegemon couldn't afford to look weak.

"Whatever helps you sleep at night," Pausanius grumbled. "Just please explain why I saw doubles of you two while we were . . . journeying here."

Sera almost laughed. She'd inputted a wrong number when calculating the warp back to prehistoric times, and they'd appeared just as their doubles were leaving the stables to go back and stop Tilda from killing Alexander the first time. Thinking about it confused even her, so she couldn't imagine what Olympias and her partner in crime thought about it.

"It'll give you something to ponder for the rest of your life," Dak answered. "With the dinosaurs. I'm kind of jealous, to be honest. Seems like a cool place. And don't worry, T. rexes don't come around these parts."

"T. rexes?" Olympias asked, looking baffled.

"Never mind."

"Come on," Sera said, stepping beside Dak and holding out the Infinity Ring. "Let's go say our final bye-bye to Aristotle." They had two more trips to make. Back to Greece, then back to the modern day, where hopefully everything was hunky-dory. Then maybe they could spend a few months healing from the toll all that time traveling took on their bodies.

Dak reached out and put his hand on the cool metal of the Ring, then he gave one last glance at the banished prisoners. "I hope you guys learned your lesson. And don't be mad at us. It was Aristotle's idea, and we just do what we're told. He's the boss of the Hystorians, you know."

Sera loved the expression of confusion that swept over the face of Olympias. She pushed the button and quantum physics took them back to Greece, far in the future and long ago, depending on how you looked at it. She just never knew how to think of such things anymore.

∞

"I don't really know what to say," Aristotle said as they sat on the balcony in the place they'd had their first deep discussion. Dak thought it seemed like thousands of years ago, which, in a way, was true. "We've been through so much in such a relatively short period of time. It's hard to say good-bye to friends. Friendship is a single soul living in two bodies. Or, in our case, four. At least I'll get to see Riq—I mean, Hephaestion—again, once the wars are over."

Dak nodded, not sure what to say himself. He was itching to get back to the modern day and make sure his parents were okay. And that the world wasn't, you know, about to blow up into tiny pieces. Sera did the talking for them.

"So, how are things going to work now?" she asked. "I know that talking about this stuff can drive you nuts, but since we corrected all the Breaks . . . then that means you don't need to start the Hystorians. But if you never start the Hystorians, how will we know to go back and . . . Oh, never mind."

Dak was glad she stopped. His head was starting to hurt.

Aristotle chuckled, a great sound coming out of the great man. He looked a million times better than he had right after the fighting.

"Not to worry, Sera. I suspect these things are simpler than we make them out to be. Most people will have no memory of the former time line, though for you two they will remain linear recollections. In fact, including your Remnants, you will have memories of three distinct time lines, in whole or in part."

Now Dak's head *really* hurt. "Boulders in the river of

time. That's what I always say when I don't have a clue what anyone's talking about."

That earned another couple of laughs, especially from Sera.

After a few moments, Aristotle grew serious. "Still, we know now that history is a special thing. And that it can be changed — but with dire consequences. I'm still going to form the Hystorians, and create a society that will last throughout the ages." He paused, scratching that grand beard of his. Then he held up a finger in true philosopher form.

"But this time things will be a little different," the old man said. "Instead of putting our focus on *changing* history, we will now do everything in our power to *protect* it. That's what we'll do, my friends. We will protect history until our last, dying breaths."

Dak wanted to high-five the guy, right there on the spot. But instead he hugged him.

Then came the good-byes, along with more tears.

The Final Remnant

TO THE future they went.

They warped to the Hystorian headquarters first. But . . . it wasn't there. Instead, all they saw was a big field, lined with rows of corn.

So they zapped themselves nearby to Sera's house next. Half of her was terrified to discover what awaited her in this new world, and the other half could hardly stand the wait. Dak had to break into a run to keep up with her as they made their way through the neighborhood.

"Things sure seem . . . normal," Dak said, slightly out of breath.

"Yeah. They do. And it's weird about the Hystorians being gone." But everything around them seemed brighter, the people happier, the colors and edges sharper. So far they hadn't seen one sign of destruction or oppression.

"I bet they still exist in some way," Dak responded. "Maybe they're a lot smaller now, without the SQ to fight. I don't know. But it sure looks like we re-created a pretty good planet, if I do say so myself."

Sera slapped him on the back. "Say it all you want. By jove, I think we've done it."

Dak whacked her on the shoulder, though not as hard. "You know, funny that you say that. The phrase 'by jove' originated in . . ." He trailed off, his face showing that he'd just been kidding. Although she honestly missed his constant spewing of historical facts. She hoped he relearned everything quickly so he could get back to it.

And then they were there. Her house. Where her uncle had raised her but she'd felt a thousand Remnants that her parents would arrive at any second.

"They're alive," Dak said, standing by her just as he'd always done. "I know it."

She nodded, then let instinct take over. The next few minutes were like a dream, as if the Remnants of her past were slowly unfolding to her like a storybook.

The front door was locked.

They rang the doorbell. No one answered.

They went around the back.

Through the yard.

Down the little dusty lane.

A long, beautiful, dreamy walk.

To the barn. That barn way behind the house.

And the doors opened.

And out they came.

Her mom.

Her dad.

Smiling.

Talking.

Laughing.

When they saw her, she bolted into a run, crossing the grassy distance faster than any horse ever could. They were shocked at her excitement when she hugged them fiercely, kissed them, laughed, and cried.

"My goodness," her mom said, pulling back and looking delightedly at her daughter. "What in the world has come over you?"

"I just missed you is all," Sera said. "I just missed you so much."

∞

The day had been a total blur for Dak.

Everything had changed, yet in some ways, it all felt the same, too. There was something perfect about it, and he felt happier than he had in a long time.

After the incredible reunion between Sera and her parents—he was man enough to admit it, he'd gotten a bit choked up—they'd walked over to Dak's house, where his own mom and dad were busy in the lab, working on twenty projects at once. It was a huge relief when he saw them alive and well. But what really made him happy was that they were doing what they loved—solving the world's problems, one by one.

The Smyths and the Frostes had actually joined forces, forming a company to seek out, discover, and invent practical scientific solutions to everything from illness to environmental issues. Their company was called Solving Quantum Physics.

Yep, Dak thought. *The SQP.* He thought that was just about the best thing ever.

"Dak."

It was Sera, pulling him back to the real world. They were sitting on a big branch of their favorite tree, enjoying the cool air and the *cleanness* of it, drinking juice. She had a tablet out, scrolling through some article with taps of her fingers. It had caught her interest big-time, judging by the look of her eyes.

"So?" he asked. "What did you find?"

"Oh, you know. Just checking out the history of Alexander the Great. That's right, the *Great*. And his best friend, Hephaestion."

Dak's jaw dropped. "What? Yeah, right."

"I'm serious! Look for yourself. It's in the *Encyclopedia Britannica.*"

Dak took the tablet from her and read through the article she'd found. He couldn't believe it. He absolutely couldn't believe it. Alexander and his armies had crossed the world, fighting when they had to, but also bringing food and knowledge and resources to countless people. Riq — renamed Hephaestion by Alexander himself — had become a dear friend and confidant to the hegemon. He was thought by many to be the true force behind the king maintaining respect for other cultures at the same time as advancing the world in the greatest leap yet in human history. They called it the Iron Empire.

Riq.

Hephaestion.

Bestie to Alexander the Great.

Dak realized he'd been holding his breath, and he let out a long and loud exhale. "That's the single coolest thing I've ever read in my entire life. Our boy did pretty well, huh? That's our boy!"

Sera laughed, and Dak loved the sound of it. They'd come so close, so many times, to everything being ruined. To death. To the end of the world. It was good to be home again. It was really, really good.

"So, what do we do with this thing?" Sera asked. She held up the satchel, the shape of the Infinity Ring obvious through the cloth.

Dak stared at it for a long time, as if the answer might appear in the stitches. "I don't know. I think once my head doesn't feel like it got beaten by a hammer from warping so much, I might be tempted to go hang out in ancient Rome for a few days."

Sera shook her head. "I know you're kidding, but we really can't do that. It seems like the world is in pretty good shape, and we better not mess it up."

"So, what are you saying? That we should destroy it? Like Riq did with Tilda's Eternity Ring?"

"No, no, no. No way. Who knows what might happen in the future. Or . . . the past?"

"Yeah," Dak agreed. "We're safe for now, but you never know. So let's decide where to put the Ring."

Sera shrugged. "I guess we can wrap it in plastic, put

it in a box, bury it. I say we give normal life a chance for a while. Sound good?"

"Sounds good times infinity."

They were silent for a while, listening to birds and wind and rustling leaves. The branch swayed a little, making Dak sleepy. It'd be nice to take a nap and not worry if the world might end the next day.

"It was fun, huh?" Sera finally said.

Dak looked at her. His best friend. "Yeah, it was. Not that I'd want to do it again."

"Me, neither. But I'll never forget what we did."

"Save the world?" Dak asked.

"Yep, save the world. And I'm glad it was with you."

She smiled then, and Dak decided not to say anything back. Sometimes words just weren't enough.

EPILOGUE

Golden

TILDA SAT, crouched, withered, dying, in the filthy corner of the alley. All of majestic Athens rose up around her, but no one cared about the sad little woman with the hair that once shone like flames. Now it was dull and lifeless and limp, like the last dying embers of a once mighty fire.

She huddled, cold despite the heat. Hungry despite the rat she'd just eaten. Shivering, she leaned against the wall and wept. Every day she'd cried, hopeless and hating the world. Hating the Hystorians. Hating that boy. That girl. That other boy.

They'd done this to her. They'd ruined her. They'd ruined her future.

Oh, how she hated them.

But it didn't matter. It was over. Though not gracious in defeat, she at least knew she'd been beaten. The SQ was no more.

And so, she'd wait.

She'd wait for death.

The next day, it still hadn't come.

That evening, a light flashed nearby, accompanied by the crackling sounds of thunder and sparks. Wind rushed through the alley, picking up leaves and trash, pelting her body. Then a sudden darkness blossomed, making her feel as if she'd been cast into a dungeon. Scared, she shifted, trying to shrink farther into the corner.

The shadow of a man stood before her. It took a while, but her eyes adjusted, and she could finally see him, standing there, silent and watchful. He was bald, and hideous scars marked his face. He wore a robe, its hood pulled down around his shoulders. And there was something terribly wrong with one of his eyes, though she couldn't quite see well enough to know for sure.

"Who are you?" she asked in a rasp, her throat dry as decayed bones.

The man sank toward the ground and knelt before her. That eye. She could see it now. Bloodshot and puffy, like it was riddled with disease.

"My name doesn't matter," he answered, his voice deep. "I'm a descendant of Ilsa, the only name we speak."

"Ilsa?" Tilda repeated.

"Yes. I have something to show you."

The man pulled out a metallic object, shining golden even in the scant light. Tilda recognized the shape—the sign for infinity. Her heart leapt back to life, consumed with so much joy she worried of dying, right there in the alley, the victim of too much emotion at once.

"What . . . how?" she sputtered, confusion threatening to destroy her elation at seeing the device.

The man spoke with soothing tones. "Ilsa commanded her posterity to study the sciences, find a way to travel through time. And we've done it. And you, Tilda, *you* are our first mission. I was sent here to get you." He reached out and gently helped her stand up, his touch bringing a warmth she hadn't felt in a long time.

"Thank you," she said, too dazed to find any other words.

"Come," he said, holding out the golden device for her to grasp. "We need you to show us the way."